The Man Who Was
Three Jumps Ahead

 AN INNER SANCTUM MYSTERY

by Hampton Stone

SIMON AND SCHUSTER • NEW YORK

1959

LIBRARY OF CONGRESS CATALOG CARD NUMBER: 59-13149
MANUFACTURED IN THE UNITED STATES OF AMERICA
BY AMERICAN BOOK-STRATFORD PRESS, NEW YORK, N. Y.

For H. W. Hewett-Thayer—
scholar, teacher, gentleman, friend—
with gratitude and affection

One

For us BUD BRONSON was no novelty. We had known him long and well, and if there was anything about him that might have slipped our minds, we could always go to his record. We had an exhaustive record on Bud Bronson.

It wasn't the longest record available to us in the New York County DA's office, and its list of crimes and misdemeanors was by no means the most heinous, but Bud Bronson, after all, had only just celebrated his twenty-fifth birthday and the only grass he'd ever allowed to grow under his feet had grown while he'd been on a State farm for juvenile offenders. With characters like Bud Bronson nothing is needed but time. There comes the day when, if we're not bringing somebody to trial for the murder of Bud Bronson, we're bringing Bud himself to trial for the murder of somebody.

That had always been so much in the cards that, any

time we had a murder in the right circles, it had become standard operating procedure to have Bud Bronson picked up for questioning. It was the thing to do but we never went through one of those sessions without wondering why we bothered. Bud Bronson didn't like the law. He didn't like cops, and he didn't like our office. The thought had never entered my mind that he might have some sort of well-concealed liking for either Assistant District Attorney Jeremiah X. Gibson or for myself. The DA had made a team of us, Gibby and me, and our team had never done any better than any of the other Assistant DAs at persuading Bud Bronson to vocalize.

Bud Bronson was nobody's stoolie. He was also nobody's patsy. I remember once, toward the end of a long and fruitless session with him, Gibby, in exasperation, asked him if it was raining outside.

"Don't ask me," Bronson said. "I don't know nothing."

That was the way he'd always been. He was careful about incriminating even the weatherman.

Then came that Saturday night. Gibby and I had been on a rough investigation. We'd run into a lot of night work with it and there was no telling how long it was going to keep us tied up. Then quite suddenly, we stumbled into one of those crazy breaks and here it was only Saturday afternoon and we had everything sewed up and not a chance that even the Old Man would throw anything fresh at us before Monday.

It was a Saturday night dropped from heaven and we were making a good try at finding some way of not wasting it. Gibby called every last number on the better pages of his address book. I called every last number I had anywhere in mine. I was still at it after Gibby had given up. That's as good a way as any of giving you the line on us. Gibby is brilliant. I am dogged.

I'd come as far down the list as Claire and even she wanted more notice than that for a Saturday night. She already had a date, but she made me promise over and over again that I'd try her another time and very soon. I finally broke loose from that and picked up the book again to see what other number I might find down there in the kennel section.

Gibby stopped me. "Claire?" he asked.

"That was Claire I just talked to. She has a date."

"She's a dog."

"This is Saturday and it's almost seven o'clock. What do you expect to find on the loose this late on a Saturday? Peacocks?"

"I'd hoped for a peahen, but let's give it up, Mac. When even the dogs have dates, you go to a show or you tie one on or you find a poker game."

We went to a show and after it we hit a bar or two. Have you ever done that on a Saturday night? You find lonely guys leaning against bars and they are a depressing lot. We said to hell with it and went home before they could depress us too much. We share an apartment, Gibby and I, and, heading for it that night, we were telling each other that it was a pleasant sort of apartment and a pity we didn't get to sit around in it more and what was wrong with fixing ourselves some drinks and getting a little mileage out of our rent money?

Call it the night when nothing worked out for us. This

place we have is a couple of upper floors in a converted brownstone and it hasn't been so much converted that it doesn't still have the old front steps. We pulled up in a cab and there was a man sitting on the steps. He was lighting a cigarette. We piled out and paid off the cabby. The man on the steps hauled to his feet and, without even having had the first drag on it, he flipped his cigarette away. He was waiting for us when we came away from the cab.

"Hi," he said. "You remember me? Bronson?"

"Yeah," I muttered.

I remembered him. I also remembered that this was a free Saturday night. All right. It hadn't panned out for any wild gaiety; but, dim as it was, it had been going several cuts better than a busman's holiday.

"Bud Bronson," Gibby said. "You're the cat who doesn't want to be remembered. Every time we or the cops remember you, it hurts your feelings."

"Don't give me no hard time now," Bronson growled. "I got information for you."

"That," I said, "will be the day."

"Anyhow," Gibby said, "it's a switch. What's on your mind?"

"The cops, they're going to be picking me up any time now," Bronson began.

"And you figured that to mean we'd be questioning you," Gibby said, "and you just couldn't wait."

Bronson scowled. I knew that scowl. It always showed up just before he'd suggest that we go and commit an anatomical impossibility on ourselves. This time he did it differently. He worked at erasing the scowl and he replaced it with a look I'd never expected I'd see on that broad, red pan of his. It was a placating look. It was even a wheedling look.

"Man," he said. "I'm asking you. You ever know me to sing?"

"No," I told him. "You're the unmusical type."

"Look," he pleaded. "You ain't got to clown it up. I got troubles. Other people, they got troubles, they go to you. You go whipping into action. All right, I got troubles. I come to you. What makes me so different?"

"The cops are going to be picking you up any time now," I said. "What do you expect us to do about it? Make a deal?"

"No deals. For a deal I know where to go. I don't go to you two."

"That," Gibby told him, "is the nicest thing you ever said to us. What are the cops picking you up for?"

"Breaking and entering."

"That's never been your line."

"Coming to you with information, that's never been my line neither, but now I'm doing it."

"He's turning all the new leaves at once," I said to Gibby.

Gibby shrugged. "Without half trying he can be more fun than Claire," he said. "Can we spare him a drink?"

"I'm on the wagon," Bronson said. "I just got to talk to you and you got to listen. What I'm talking about, it's a snatch. It's got to be a snatch."

"And that's much more in your line than breaking and entering," Gibby said. "All right. Come on upstairs. We'll listen."

5

We went up to the apartment and I fixed drinks, but it was just for Gibby and myself. Bronson wasn't climbing off the wagon. He did say he'd take a Coke maybe if we had one but we didn't and he said he hadn't wanted it anyway.

Indoors, where we had a proper light on him, we could see how deep his switch went. This was hardly the Bud Bronson we'd known. I couldn't count how many times we'd worked really hard at sweating him. Now when we weren't working at it at all, Bronson was sweating. This bird, out of whom we'd never succeeded in wringing even a single drop, was sweating on his own.

Everything about the guy was changed. I'd never seen him so thoroughly shaved and barbered. I'd never seen him so neatly and soberly dressed. Dark-blue suit, white shirt, dark-blue necktie—he looked like graduation day at Central High.

"You know what night of the week this is?" he began.

"Skip the calendar," I said. "What's with a snatch?"

"Saturday night always they go out; and the chick, she's always got a Saturday night date. Nobody went out tonight. Nobody had no dates and it ain't like they been having company in or like that. Nobody, not even the doctor, and the missus looking like she can use a doctor and having one all the time when she ain't even like she is tonight. And that ain't all. They don't go to bed. They got lights on all over the house and they say Dora, she ain't in, and that's damn funny because she's never had a Saturday night off and she's told me a million times not to look for it. She can't get it, because Saturday night they always go out and she's got to be in."

"Who's Dora?" Gibby asked.

All this stuff had been pouring out of Bronson. It needed a lot more names and a lot of organization.

"Dora's my dame," Bronson said stoutly. His manner made it evident that he stood ready to demolish the first man who might venture to challenge that. "It's on account of Dora I'm on the wagon. It's on account of her I went out and got me this suit and the plain necktie and the plain shirt. It's on account of Dora I'm working steady."

I laughed. "All that for Dora," I said, "and even so she'd never give you a Saturday night date. So now you go around on a Saturday night and somebody's beaten your time. She is out but with some other guy. That's life. That's women. It happens all the time. Relax."

He didn't relax. He balled up his fists and he breathed hard.

"You was anyone else," he moaned, "I'd cream you for saying even the half of that."

"It happens to the best of us," I said. "Look right here. Me. Saturday night and I couldn't find myself a date. Mr. Gibson, he couldn't find a Saturday night date either. There'll be other Saturdays, other dames. They stand you up and go out with some other guy, it's because they want to. They don't have to be kidnaped for it. So get smart and forget all this stuff about yelling 'snatch' and get down to cases. What's with your breaking and entering rap?"

"Don't cheer, boys," Gibby murmured. "Those men are dying."

"What's with the double-talk?" Bronson wailed. "Tell me plain. You want to listen to me or don't you?"

7

"I'm all ears," Gibby said, "but I can't say I've been hearing much. Dora's your dame and she can never go out with you on a Saturday night date but you go around and give it the try anyhow. Someone comes to the door and says Dora is out and you blow your stack and go around and climb in by a window or something boyish and impulsive like that for which the cops are now after you. The idea seems to be that if you get to tell us your sad story before we get to see anything like the formal complaint, we might put in some sort of a fix for you. Now what ever gave you the idea we operate that way and what ever gave you the idea we'd want to? Do we owe you a favor or something?"

"You don't owe me nothing and I don't owe you nothing. Me—I know all of you, cops, DAs, the whole sonofabitching works. I always figure it can never happen to me, not to me, Bud Bronson, but it's happened. I'm in trouble; it's the kind of trouble I need one of you sonofabitches. So maybe I can have it that it's a smart one at least; and the smart one, that's you."

"Thanks," Gibby said. "I'm this smart. I know you never gave me a damn thing I can use, but it was always a matter of that's the way it goes. The boys bring you in. We try to get you to talk. You don't. You don't want to. That I understand because, as you say, I'm a smart sonofabitch; but this time it's the switch. Remember? Nobody brought you in this time. You came looking for us. You're volunteering information, but you're still not giving us a damn thing we can use."

"I told you it was a snatch, her and Lonnie."

"Her? That's still Dora?"

8

"Yeah, Dora and Little Lonnie."

"And Dora's your dame and who's Little Lonnie?"

"The baby. That's her job, Lonnie, the baby. She fixes his bottles for him. She gives him his bath. She dresses him. She undresses him. She takes him out to the goddamn park. She changes his goddamn diapers."

"Then Dora's a baby nurse? Is that it?"

"I been telling you."

"Okay. Where does she work?"

"For them people on East Sixty-second. Hulon B. Stewart. The baby, they call him Lonnie. That's for Hulon B., Junior."

"The Stewarts always go out on Saturday night and Dora has to stay on the job with the baby. What made tonight different? What were you doing over there?"

"What made it different is they say she ain't there."

"What gave you the idea of checking up on her?"

"No idea of checking up on her. This is Saturday like any Saturday. She can't go out, so I go there and I stay in with her. The kid hollers, she goes to him. He don't wake up, she don't have to go to him. We're together like that every Saturday night and a lot of the other nights she can't come out. That's what's different tonight."

"Nights she can go out," Gibby murmured thoughtfully, "you have a date with her. Nights she can't go out, you go over there and help her baby-sit. It's a seven-day week and completely monogamous."

"It ain't monotonous," Bronson said heatedly. "Dora's my dame. It's the real thing."

"I bet," Gibby said. "How do you do with the diapering?"

9

Bronson started for the door. Nobody made any move to stop him. With a hand on the doorknob he stopped himself.

"Look," he said plaintively. "Look. You got to do something. You can't just sit here making funny."

"Get to the breaking and entering," I suggested.

Gibby overruled me. "Don't hurry it," he said. "On this, even if we know everything, we aren't going to know much." He turned to Bronson. "Come back and sit down, Bud," he said. "When did you see your dame last?"

"Yesterday. Last night. We had a date last night."

"Like any other date?"

"Like any other date with her."

Bronson wasn't going to have us think that a date with Dora could be like a date with any other babe. This was special.

"That's what I meant," Gibby said. "No fight or anything like that?"

"No."

"Nothing funny or different about the way she acted?"

"Nothing. Like always."

"You didn't hit her or do anything else that maybe would make her mad?"

"I never hit no dame in my life, not even dames they weren't Dora."

"Nothing else to make her mad?"

"She wasn't mad. There wasn't nothing like that."

"How have you been doing with this Dora?"

"I been doing all right."

"Been laying her?"

"She lets me kiss her a little. I prove to her I can go

straight. You know, keep a job, stay on the wagon, keep out of trouble, hold it that way for one whole, solid year. I can do that, she's going to marry me. That's the way it is with me and Dora. She's wearing the ring I give her and it ain't even a hot ring. I walked into the store with her and I bought the ring, paying out on it every week."

"Is this a dame," Gibby asked, "or a probation officer?"

"She's a dame she won't marry no mugg."

"Sure you didn't step out of line last night? Something like making the kind of pass Dora won't hold still for?"

"I told you no."

"It doesn't have to be anything with any harm in it. When a dame's the way you say this Dora is even a little bit of rape can do it."

"Don't I know it? Back when I first knew her I tried once to push her over. She swung on me with her pocketbook. You can still see the place."

He had thick, dark hair with quite a bit of curl in it. He pushed back a curl from his forehead to display a thread of scar that ran for almost two inches along the hair line.

"She do that with a pocketbook?" Gibby asked.

"It's a pocketbook with a long strap on it," Bronson explained. "You know like they carry hanging from their shoulder? It's got a bar of metal clean across the top of it where it closes. She holds it by the end of the strap and she gives it a full swing, it cuts a guy's head open. So I'm down on my butt and the blood running down on my face and she looks at me and tells me that if I ever lay a hand on her again, she'll do it a couple of inches lower and cut a goddamn eye out. I had to have stitches there in my head and I was five weeks getting her even to let me talk to her again. I learned it back there at the beginning."

"And you think she's been snatched," Gibby mused, "a dame who can handle herself like that."

"She doesn't sound like the victim type," I observed.

"Somebody pulls a heater on her," Bronson growled. "It can happen to anybody."

"Somebody pulled a heater on her?" Gibby asked.

"Nobody's going to get her and the kid by just grabbing her by the arm."

Gibby led him along and he gave us the complete details on it. They'd had a date the previous night and it had been like all their other dates. It had in fact been among their better grade dates since it had been pay day and Bronson had been able to show his Dora his savings bank passbook with the fresh deposit entry in it. On those days when he could show her that he had added to his savings, she would always be well pleased with him and they would always have a happy time. He had brought her home and she had allowed him to kiss her good night.

"I said, 'See you tomorrow, baby,'" Bronson told us. "She said, 'See you tomorrow, Lawrence.' She always calls me Lawrence. She don't never call me Bud or even Larry. She says it ain't dignified."

"I see," Gibby said. "You had a nice evening and you parted in affection and dignity with a promise on both sides to see each other again tonight."

Bronson accepted Gibby's description. It was evident

that he felt it fitted the circumstances to a nicety. He also felt it was a complete impossibility that Dora, having parted with the understanding that he would be over the following night, would, even in the most unlikely event of a change of plans, have gone off without waiting for him or without at least leaving him some message.

"She'd have given me a ring and told me or something," he said.

"Other times it happened she did phone you and tell you not to come?"

"They was no other times, but I know her. She's that way about promising. She says 'see you.' I say 'see you.' That's a promise. She don't walk out on it and not even leave me some word."

He'd gone around to see her just as he had every other Saturday evening. Promptly at eight he'd rung the bell at the basement entrance of the house in Sixty-second Street. Even then he had noticed that the house didn't look as it had looked other Saturday nights. It was a blaze of light. From top to bottom, it showed not a single dark window.

"Sometimes they're giving a party," he said, "they got lights all over the house, but even then they's some rooms it isn't. It isn't up top where Dora and Mary, they got their rooms, and it isn't in the room where the baby, he'll be sleeping. Tonight it's everywhere."

As he told it, the peculiarities multiplied. It had never before been any member of the family who had come to answer his ring at the basement door. Mostly it had been Dora herself because she would be expecting him.

Occasionally it would be Mary, who did the cooking and cleaning.

"When Mary come," he said, "it was always because the baby had been crying or like that and Dora, she had to be upstairs getting him quiet. When it's like that, Mary opens for me and she tells me how Dora is busy for now and Dora says tell me I should come in and she'll be down soon. Mostly when it's like that, I know it even before Mary comes to the door or says anything. I can hear the baby yelling upstairs."

It hadn't been Mary who had come to the door and there had been no sound of a baby's crying.

"It was the babe come to open the door and Mr. Stewart himself, he's right there behind her. They know me from the nights I come and stay with Dora, when they're going out. They tell me Dora's had to go out and I figure it's all right. Maybe she's run around to the avenue to pick something up at the drugstore or like that. I ask can I wait for her. They say she's out for the evening. I ask did she leave me some word. They say no. I ask can I talk to Mary. She'd have left me the word with Mary. The chick says Mary is busy. I say maybe she can go ask Mary. She says sure, but Mr. Stewart, he gets hard. He says I been told and what am I hanging around bothering them for. I been told she ain't there and she ain't left no message and I'm to get the hell out and stop bothering people."

Bronson made it clear that ordinarily this was no answer he would have taken, but that this time he had taken it. He had been inhibited by the thought of Dora's wrath. She would never stand for him giving Mr. Stewart any lip. Gibby tossed a couple of questions in just to keep things straight in the who's who department. Bronson cleared up the reference to the chick. The chick was Emily Stewart, daughter of the house.

"She's his daughter," Bronson explained. "Not hers, just his. It's his second wife and she ain't any older than the daughter, maybe even younger a little."

Bronson had given up on his insistence that he wanted a word with Mary, the other maid, but he hadn't gone away. He had stayed within sight of the house and he had watched. After about fifteen minutes he saw Mary through the basement windows. She had come down to the kitchen for something. Thinking that he could speak to her then, he had again gone to the basement door and put his finger on the bell.

"This time," he said, "Mary does come to the door but I hardly get to ask her before he's tearing down the stairs; and he sees it's me, he's right away raising hell. He already told me Dora she ain't there. Is he going to have to throw me out?"

There had been enough time for Mary to tell him Dora wasn't home and that she'd left no message, but then Stewart had been upon them and there had been time for nothing more. Bud had walked around the block and then had come back and watched the house. It was then that he had been so much impressed with the house being lighted throughout. He had concentrated on the lights in the baby's room.

"I know that kid," he said. "It's a kid he cries a lot. It's getting later all the time and if the kid's asleep, there ain't going to be all that light going in his room, and that kid if he ain't asleep, he's yelling, except that he isn't. They ain't a sound coming out of that room of his upstairs."

He watched the house for an hour, enough time to get him past being angry and to bring him around to being uneasy. The Stewarts didn't go out. Their daughter didn't go out. They had no visitors. Nobody came or went. The whole house blazed with light, but not a sound came out of it. The infant never cried.

One of the first-story windows stood open. It had come to be about ten o'clock and the street had gone quiet and deserted. It was too much for Bronson. For an hour he had been studying the face of the house and he knew exactly how he could climb up the wall and reach that open window. He climbed it.

Coming in by the window, he spent a half hour in the house. He crept from room to room, guiding himself by the sound of voices, avoiding the occupied rooms but checking all the others.

"I got upstairs," he told us, "and I looked in Dora's room. She ain't there. They ain't nobody there. I looked in her closet, and her uniform it ain't there. You know, what she wears to take the baby to the park and like that. If that ain't in her closet, it's got to mean she's out with the kid, but ten o'clock at night. She don't take no kid airing in no park at ten o'clock at night. I go down and look in the kid's room. Nobody there neither. No kid, nobody. The room right next to it, that's their room, Stewart and the missus. I can hear them in there, so I stand by the door and listen. She's in there crying and he's trying to talk to her. That's how I know it's got to be a snatch. I know it from what they're saying."

He gave us the direct quote on what he'd heard and, even though this was Bud Bronson from whom we were having it, I found myself compelled to believe him. He'd heard Mrs. Stewart moan about her baby, her poor, lost baby she would never see again. Then Stewart had tried to comfort her. He'd told her not to say that, not even to think it. He'd promised her the boy would be all right. They'd be bringing him home on Monday.

"Then she screams at him," Bronson told us. " 'Monday,' she screams. 'Two whole days. You'll wait two whole days. What are you made of that you can wait two whole days? Are they taking care of him? Have they got his formula right? Is he being hurt? Is he being frightened? Two whole days you'll let them keep him. What are you made of?' "

"What was he saying to all this?" Gibby asked.

"He says he's made of flesh and blood just like she is. He says he's suffering just like she is. He says what can he do. He's helpless. His hands is tied. It's Saturday. Where can he go Saturday night and lay his hands on five hundred grand cash money? Even Monday, when banks'll be open, he says it ain't going to be no pipe, getting a half million together in cash all that quick. They's a good chance he'll be ruining himself doing it, but he's going to do it, except he can't before Monday. He can't before they open the banks. He tells her five hundred grand is a lot of money, more than anybody keeps laying around the house; and she screams at him what's money. What's he thinking about, money or his baby? Then she's moaning again about her baby alone in the hands of strangers and he tells her the kid's got Dora with him and how she knows Dora's a good girl and how Dora really loves that kid and she ain't going to let nothing happen to him she can help. He tells her she shouldn't worry the kid'll be getting the right formula and all that because Dora's there and Dora knows more about the formula than she ever knew. That gets her to screaming at him again. She screams that he's blaming her, that he thinks she had ought to have always been with the kid instead of leaving him with no nurse. That's where the chick takes a hand. The chick tells her Daddy never said that. She tells her nobody thinks it's anyone's fault. She works on her she should take some sleeping pills and quiet down."

Bronson fell silent and none of us said anything for a full minute while Gibby studied the man. Then Gibby did break the silence.

"And that's all of it?" he asked.

"Ain't it enough? They can't get the kid back till Monday because he can't get no five hundred grand in cash money before the banks open. He don't know how he's going to do it even then but he's going to do it. What's that if it ain't a snatch? Dora and the baby both."

"Okay," Gibby said. "How did you get out of the house?"

"Same way I come in. Nobody seen me, but I pulled myself up to that window going in. I hang from that window and drop going out. I got fingerprints all over that window sill."

"You didn't take anything?"

18

"Take anything?" Bronson was outraged. "It's a snatch and they've got my girl, whoever's done it. What'll I be taking? I ask you. What'll I be taking?"

"You went in about ten and you were in there a half hour. That would make it about ten-thirty. What did you do after that? Come over here to wait for us? You lost a couple of hours that way. Why didn't you go straight to the police?"

"Look," Bronson moaned. "Look, Mr. Gibson. You ain't that kind of a square. I go to the cops. Me, Bud Bronson. I tell them what I told you. How far do I get? Can you picture me going to the cops and telling them I been climbing in people's windows?"

"I couldn't picture you coming to us either."

"You think I wanted to? You ask me what I done after I got out of the place. You know what I done? I went around to guys I know. I asked questions. I ask where's this guy, has anybody heard of him being around. He ain't around. He got picked up two months ago in Kansas and they got him out there waiting for trial. I ask what a certain mob's doing right now and they ain't a one of them in town. They got something going for them down in Havana, between Havana and Key West. They're all down there and it's a big operation. They're taking guys in all the time and moving them down there. They need all the men they can get. This is new people, Mr. Gibson. This ain't nobody you'll know or the cops'll know or anybody's going to know. It's new people. Believe me, if it wasn't, I'd never have come to you. But it's nobody I can reach, so it's got to be some new punks and

19

you know how it is with them new ones. Something scares them or like that, they'll do anything.

"Stewart, he can wait till Monday. He can go to the banks and get his five hundred grand. He can maybe even get his baby back. A baby can't go remembering where he was took. A baby can't go picking nobody out of no line-up. A baby can't get on no witness stand and say him and him and him. They done it. Stewart can maybe get his baby back for five hundred grand, but what about Dora? What gets her back? That's what I want to know. What gets Dora back?"

Two

WE WENT AROUND to Sixty-second Street and we took Bronson with us. The house was exactly as he had described it. Ablaze with lights from top to bottom, it had a festive look; but it was silent, uncannily so.

We were most unwelcome, but that was to have been expected. Turn up on a man's doorstep well after one o'clock in the morning. Have in tow a character like Bud Bronson whom your householder has found troublesome previously that night. Announce yourself as a couple of Assistant District Attorneys and tell the man that you have come to help him. The least he's going to tell you is that he didn't ask for help.

Gibby rang the bell. It was answered quickly and the answering couldn't have been more exactly like Bronson's account of it. A young woman opened the door. She was white-faced. She had chewed all the lipstick off her mouth. Her eyes were wide and feverish. As soon as she had the door open, she whipped her hands behind her back. I could guess it was in the hope that we wouldn't see she was shaking. It was no good. This was a frightened girl and it showed.

Coming up right behind her was a man. He was in shirt sleeves and he had pulled his collar open and had his necktie hanging loose. He was red-eyed and he was sweating. In his middle or late forties, he had the ruddy look of good health that should have made him look younger. There were other signs about him. His necktie, a foolish pair of red suspenders he was wearing, the way he had his hair cut—there was something aggressively young about all that. This was a man who worked at being as young as he ever was and there had probably been other nights when he could have put it over. This night he had been through the wringer and that showed, too.

They both spotted Bronson right off. The girl, talking right past us, spoke to him.

"Now, look," she said. "You don't think you can come here and see Dora this time of night. What's the matter with you? Are you drunk?"

Bronson said nothing. He was leaving it to us, but we didn't get to say anything either. The man pulled the girl away from the door.

"It's all right, Emmy," he said. "Go back upstairs. Go to Gloria. I'll handle this."

"Mr. Stewart?" Gibby began.

The man waved him off. He was waiting for the girl to go. She didn't move.

"Gloria needs . . ." he began, but with a look in our direction he bit it off, leaving it with a look of mute appeal he tossed at the girl. She gave it the don't-see-and-don't-hear treatment, but it was obvious that it was the treatment. She didn't want any part of being sent off to look after Gloria.

"We're from the District Attorney's office, Mr. Stewart," Gibby said, trying again.

Stewart went white. He tried to speak but he couldn't make his voice come. The girl spoke for him.

"What do you want?" she asked.

"You need help," Gibby said. "You need all the help you can get. We're on your side."

Stewart found his voice. "A nursemaid's boy friend," he said scornfully, "begins to be troublesome. That's an annoyance, but I do think we can handle it without help from anyone."

"Monday," Gibby said, "after the banks have opened and after you've managed to raise half a million dollars, which is likely to take a little time even when the banks are open. Do you really think it's safe to wait that long?"

"Are you all drunk?" Stewart asked.

"Kidnaping," Gibby said. "Don't try to handle it alone, man."

Stewart, looking more panicked than ever, made a shushing gesture.

"Come in," he said. "Come in for God's sake. Don't stand out there where anybody might see you."

Emily forgot about hiding her shakes from us. "Daddy," she moaned. "Are you crazy, Daddy? You had trouble getting rid of him before. Why ask for it now? The others say they're from the District Attorney's office, but how do you know they are? We don't want any of them in the house, Daddy."

"Worse having them hanging about outside where they can be seen," Stewart whispered.

"Daddy," Emily begged. "Please. It's a mistake."

"I didn't want it this way," Stewart groaned. "I'm just trying to minimize the . . ." With a glance at us he bit it off without putting a word to what it was he wanted to minimize.

"You've heard from them," Gibby said. "They've made the usual threats. Don't go near the police if you ever want to see your baby again. Don't bring the cops into this if you want your baby to live."

We had stepped into the house and Bronson had followed after us. Now Stewart darted around us to slam the door shut. The girl grabbed that moment to get her own licks in.

"You're talking the most ridiculous nonsense," she said, raging at us helplessly. "I don't know what you want or what you're up to, but I can't believe you're from the District Attorney's office at all. If you don't leave here at once and stop bothering us, I shall call the police."

"Even if the people who are holding Little Lonnie think you are calling about them?" Gibby asked. "We're in plain clothes and we came quietly. Do you really want uniformed officers in prowl cars with the sirens going?"

"Emily," Stewart shouted. "I told you to go to Gloria. I'm handling this."

"Gloria doesn't need me," the girl said. "She doesn't want me." The girl started to cry.

Stewart patted her shoulder and said no more about Gloria. He turned back to us.

"Gentlemen," he said. "Come inside. Let me give you a drink. I'm sure we can clear up this misunderstanding."

"You haven't even asked to see their credentials," Emily whispered, drying her eyes.

That was all right. We brought out our identification and showed it. Stewart gave the cards only a hasty glance. Emily studied them. Bronson, while the Stewarts were busy with our credentials, slipped off into a front room that opened from the hall we were standing in. Stewart showed us into the room after Bronson.

When we came in, Bronson was at an open window. He had his hands on the sill and he was leaning out.

"Come away from there. Damn you," Stewart snarled at him.

Bronson brought his head in. Carefully he dusted off the palms of his hands and then he examined them to see if he had cleared them of any soot he might have picked up from the window ledge.

"I'm just closing the window," he said. "We don't want nobody outside hearing us."

He pulled the window shut. Stewart buttoned the collar of his shirt and pulled the knot of his tie up.

"Name your poison, gentlemen," he said, giving jocularity the good old try. It was so hollow it echoed.

"No, thanks," I said.

"Not on duty," Gibby added.

Stewart forced a smile. "Duty?" he murmured. "What duty can you possibly have with a law-abiding taxpayer?"

"Mr. Bronson," I said, "came to us with information. It's our duty to investigate it."

"Gentlemen," Stewart said. "Mr. Bronson is a friend of Dora Mason. Miss Mason is employed by us in the capacity of nursemaid. She takes care of my infant son. On evenings when Dora does not have time off she has been permitted to entertain Mr. Bronson here. Mr. Bronson expected to be so entertained tonight. He was not aware that Dora has the night off; and, apparently learning that she is off tonight has been a serious shock to him. He has my sympathy, but we've all taken our bumps somewhere along the path of true love. I can remember taking mine, gentlemen, but it was never the occasion for any investigation by the District Attorney's office."

Gibby shook his head. "Mr. Bronson," he said, "knew what he was doing when he shut that window before we started talking. You are overwrought, sir, and with the best of reasons. Probably none of you have any idea of how much your voices have been getting out of control. You've been screaming at each other. Earlier this evening Mr. Bronson, who was waiting outside the house in the hope that Dora would come home, heard you out in the street."

Having made that one small change in the story, Gibby went on with it, telling how Bronson had heard Mrs. Stewart cry for her baby and had heard her accuse her husband of caring more for the money than he did for his infant son. Gibby gave him the full quote on what Bronson had overheard; and, watching their faces as Gibby talked to them, I could see easily that Bud Bronson had the right of it. They looked stricken, caved in. The girl was making a desperate fight for control of herself. She had already been crying, but now the tears came up in Stewart's eyes. He mumbled something feeble about hay fever.

When Gibby had delivered the whole package, he fell silent and waited for them to make the next move. Stewart blew his nose hard and mopped his eyes.

"This damn hay fever," he wailed.

Emily patted his shoulder sympathetically. "Look, Daddy," she said, "why don't you go upstairs, take some pyribenzamine, and lie down? It doesn't take two of us to clear up this misunderstanding."

"Yes, Mr. Stewart," Gibby said, slipping it in smoothly. "We don't need both of you to show us up to the baby's room. A quick look at him safely asleep in his crib and there'll be nothing left for us to do except apologize and haul out of here. We don't need either of you to show us the boy's room. Bronson here knows his way around the house. He can take us up."

"He isn't. . ." Stewart moaned.

His speech was choked and labored. The girl, having let herself cry, had now pulled herself together enough to speak for him.

"My father is right," she said with a show of spirit. "This buffoon isn't going to show anybody around the house. He's already been here twice and we had to ask him to leave. I can understand now why Dora's trying to get rid of him. She's the quietest, most decent sort of girl."

"She's better'n that," Bronson growled. "If she wants to brush me off, she'll tell me it, straight to my face. She

27

won't go sneaking out on me, not Dora. She ain't the kind goes sneaking on anything."

"The girl is out," Emily Stewart said. She was trying to make it sound firm. It sounded hysterical. "As for what this man heard, there has never been anything sillier. We're going to be in a play—Daddy and Gloria and I. He heard us rehearsing our parts. It's a foolish play, the craziest sort of melodrama and anyone who had the first bit of sense would have known that the lines were impossibly theatrical. There's that line of Daddy's. Gloria asks him what he's made of and he answers that he's made of flesh and blood just as she is. I ask you. In real life does anyone ever say anything that corny?"

"If you're asking me," Gibby answered, "I'll have to say yes. People do. That, Miss Stewart, is where the best corn grows, in real life. People under stress fall back on the well-worn phrases that come easily to the mind. They don't have the time or the mood for polishing up something original or clever."

The girl forced a laugh. "I know Daddy," she said. "Corn never comes easily to his mind. I know that if only from the rough time he's having memorizing his lines."

Gibby shrugged. "Then I guess we'll have to apologize," he said. "The baby's upstairs safely asleep. Dora Mason is out two-timing on her fiancé. You people are rehearsing a play and you have such a thing for Con Edison that even the baby sleeps with all the lights turned on in his room."

He was reaching for his hat. Bronson came storming forward.

"The baby ain't up there," he shouted. "I been . . ."

28

I had begun to wonder about Bronson. I'd caught it when we'd first come into the house. It had been Bronson who had chosen the room in which we'd been having this interview with the Stewarts. He had slipped in here, leaving the rest of us to follow him. When we had come in, he'd been at the open window and he hadn't been in the process of closing it. He had been leaning out with his two hands pressed against the window sill.

Maybe you noticed that yourself and maybe you missed it. After all, you don't have anything like our knowledge of Bud Bronson, his tricks, and his capabilities. His hands pressed against that window sill had been no inadvertence. He had known what he was doing. It had been by that window that he had come into the house earlier that night and by that window he had left. It had been on that window sill that he had left the fingerprint evidence that had been worrying him. Coming back to the house with us, it was the first thing he'd taken care of—his hands pressed against that window sill to neutralize the fingerprint evidence, and that in the presence of witnesses.

With this in mind, I was hanging back and waiting to see what Bronson's move was going to be. He could admit to the Stewarts that he had been inside the house, risking the consequences of that admission and, by taking that risk, proving that when he had come to us with his kidnaping story he had been on the up and up. He could also go on admitting nothing, and with that job he had done on the window he would be in the clear.

It would have added up to a fancy bit. I admit that, but I knew Bronson and I was ready to believe that, when it came to arranging a cover-up for himself, he could be just that fancy. It was a possibility. For reasons he hadn't seen fit to divulge to Gibby and me, Bronson had done a little job of illegal entry in this house. It had been a good job and he'd gotten away with it nicely, but there had been just that one little detail amiss and it had bothered Bud Bronson, the perfectionist. While he had been in the house, he had overheard the Stewarts in their rehearsal of their amateur theatricals and that had presented to him the irresistible opportunity. He could come to us with that story of his and he could suck us into taking him back to the house where he could take care of that one little, troublesome fingerprint detail, and do it under the eyes of a pair of impeccable witnesses.

Had our informant in this matter been anyone but Bud Bronson, I would certainly have been overwhelmed by the rest of it. The way the Stewarts—father and daughter —looked, the faltering feebleness of their protests and their rebuttals, in every detail they did seem to be unwilling corroborators of Bud Bronson's story, but there was the whole history of our past experience with Bronson. If there was anything else you could possibly believe, it just wasn't smart to believe a single word of anything Bud Bronson might tell you.

Inhibited as I was by that one touch of skepticism, I did expect that Gibby would be at least as skeptical. Between the two of us, I'm the credulous one. Many's the bill of goods I've been ready to buy when I've been saved by Gibby's sales resistance. So I was hanging back and waiting for Bronson to prove himself, and this time it was Gibby who was buying. He gave Bud no chance to tell the Stewarts where he had been. He broke in on him and took over.

"Bud's been thinking," he said, taking the words out of Bronson's mouth and substituting for them others that were rather too subtle to have come out of the Bronson mind even when it might have been at its most tricky. "He's been thinking that it's a most extraordinary coincidence that in this play you're rehearsing you talk about a character named Dora who knows how to take care of the baby. The mother in the play need have no worry about the baby's being fed the correct formula. Dora is with the baby and Dora knows the formula."

"They said Dora," Bronson said eagerly. "I heard them. They said Dora. That's what I been thinking."

"Of course it is," Gibby agreed.

"Actually," Emily Stewart said, "the name in the lines is Nora. It's just another thing that makes it that sort of play. Maids in those silly things are always called Nora or Mary, as though a girl called Phyllis or Evelyn could never get a domestic job."

"Nora—Dora," Gibby muttered. "Easily confused. What's your play called?"

He addressed the question to Hulon Stewart but he had no answer from that quarter. Stewart was busy blowing his nose. I thought unnecessarily, but I reminded myself that one never can know about hay fever.

The girl answered. "It's called *The Kidnaper*," she said.

"Who wrote it?"

"Some fool. It's really a dreadfully bad play."

"Where are you doing it?"

"It will be a private performance."

Gibby shook his head at her. "With neither the police nor the District Attorney's office invited," he said. "You've made the big try, Miss Stewart, but you aren't kidding anyone. There is no play and it wasn't a rehearsal Bronson heard. It was the real thing. We know fright when we see it and we know anxiety and grief and agony. We also know why you want no part of us tonight."

"Or any other night," the girl said. "I don't like being called a liar."

"Of course you don't," Gibby said. "Not any more than you like lying, but you have no choice. It would be so easy to tell us where Dora and the baby are tonight, and so easy to bring the script of that play out and show us the lines Bronson overheard. You could be rid of us in short order that way and you do want to be rid of us."

"We do," she wailed. "Oh, we do. You can see we're upset, but it's a family thing we don't want to discuss with strangers. You've asked your questions and you've had your answers. Now, please, leave and let us have some privacy."

"The kidnapers," Gibby said, "have been in contact. They've told you what the family is always told. You are to play along and follow instructions. If you do exactly as you are told and if you don't notify the police, the baby will be returned to you unharmed. If you go near the law or make one wrong move, you'll never see Lonnie alive again. You're trying to follow instructions. You're afraid to do anything else. Don't think we can't understand that."

"You can't understand anything," the girl screamed at

him. "You can't understand even the simplest English. We've told you you're wrong. We've told you Lonnie hasn't been kidnaped. We've explained everything, but it's as though we'd never talked to you at all."

"No," Gibby said. "It's more complicated than that. Since we've had no proper information of the kidnaping of the infant, Hulon Stewart, Jr., there isn't much we can do about that. We have, though, been informed of the kidnaping of Dora Mason and that leaves us no choice. We have to go to work on the Mason kidnaping. We came here hoping to have your help and co-operation with it. We can't pretend that we aren't working in the dark on this thing. With the information you can give us we should be a little less in the dark and we'd have a better chance of handling this without alarming the kidnapers. You see, that's always the most dangerous aspect of these kidnaping cases, the chance that someone—police, the DA's office, the family, anyone—will do something and, without even knowing what he is doing, he will scare the kidnapers. It's when they're scared that they are most dangerous."

"Nobody's been kidnaped," the girl moaned. "Go away."

"How do you think we work in a case of kidnaping?" Gibby said gently. "You seem to think we'll go all out to catch a criminal without the first thought for the life or safety of Lonnie or of Dora Mason. You're wrong about that, as wrong as you can possibly be. Our first and only consideration is and will be to do everything possible to insure the safe return of Lonnie and Dora. That has to take precedence over catching any kidnapers or bringing anyone to justice. That will be our whole purpose either way, whether we have your co-operation or not. How we handle it will be your decision. If you want to pay the ransom, if you want us to stay out of it until after the ransom has been paid and the child returned to you, you can have it that way, but not all on your own the way you're trying to do it. We've had experience with this kind of thing. We can advise you. You won't be forced to take our advice, but you should have it available."

Gibby was talking to the girl, but through her he was hammering away at her father. They were heavy blows and shrewd ones, and Hulon Stewart was wincing away from every one of them. Looking for Dora Mason, we would be blundering along in the dark. We would inevitably be making mistakes because we wouldn't know what the kidnaper's instructions had been. We wouldn't know how far we might go in safety and just which of our moves could be calculated to trigger these people who were holding the baby and Dora. The Stewarts on their side would also be blundering along in the dark.

"You're thinking that you're going to take no chances," Gibby said. "You're going to follow the instructions to the letter, and it can turn out that it is exactly the best thing you can do. Sometimes it is, but you don't know how to follow those instructions. You've had no experience. There are a million things you can do wrong. You won't mean to do any of them. You won't even know you're doing them. Certainly you won't know how they are going to be read by the kidnapers if they're watching your every move. You'll think you're doing exactly what they told you to do and there will be something, just out of your inexperience, that's going to look wrong, and that will be enough. Dora and Lonnie will be dead."

"You're wrong," Emily Stewart moaned. "We are having trouble, but it's personal, family trouble. It isn't anything criminal or legal or anything like that. Please leave us alone."

"Your father is going to have to make the decision, Miss Stewart," Gibby said. "He is going to have to decide which risk he wants to take. Lonnie is his child."

Stewart raised his head and braced himself to speak. The girl stood trembling, waiting for what he would say.

"The boy," Stewart said, "is safe. We know where he is."

Gibby shrugged. "Your decision," he said. "We'll be looking for Dora Mason. If we turn up anything that should be of concern to you, we'll be in touch."

He started from the room. He didn't even get as far as the door. Another babe came charging in from the hall, and when I'd had the thought that Emily was in bad shape, I hadn't seen anything. This one was a disaster.

The day babes took to painting their faces, there was a whole flock of things they had to give up doing. Chewing on their lips was one thing. This babe had been doing a savage job on hers. She had gnawed them bloody and, in the process, she had taken all her lipstick off the places where she had put it and smeared it over her face halfway down to her chin.

Another thing they can't do is any real job of crying. This babe was a platinum blonde, one of those with the long hair that falls over the shoulders. She'd had both of her hands in her hair and it looked as though she'd been tearing at it. It was half wet and long strands of it had come forward and were straggling all over her cheeks. That would have been bad enough in itself but there was the mascara and the eye shadow to make it worse. A gal can have mascara or she can have tears. She can't have both and keep herself any kind of a face at all.

The mascara was black and the eye shadow was green and her crying had run both in muddy trails down her cheeks to furrow her pancake make-up. Mix all that stuff up with the platinum hair and the babe looked as though she had been storing her face in a damp basement until it had broken out in mildew.

Stewart hurried to her. "Gloria," he said. "You shouldn't have come down, Gloria. Come, I'll take you back to your room."

Gloria glared at him. "Don't you come near me," she snarled. "Don't touch me. Leave me alone."

Emily tried to talk to her.

"Darling," she said. "Daddy knows what he's doing."

Gloria ignored her. "I want my baby," she wailed. She grabbed Gibby by the lapels of his coat and shook him. "Get me back my baby. I'll do anything if I can only get my baby back."

Gibby took her hands. He was very gentle with her. "Easy, Mrs. Stewart," he murmured. "Easy, now. Sit down, pull yourself together, and tell us all about it."

"You clown," Emily yelled at him, still trying desperately. "You hopeless clown. Can't you see what's wrong with her? Don't you know? She's been drinking, you fool.

Can't you see she's drunk? She doesn't know what she's saying."

It wasn't any good. Gloria knew what she was saying and she said a lot of it. She screamed it, in fact. The words she used she could have learned only in a tough school and they came tumbling to her lips. It was obvious that she didn't have to reach for them. She had words for her husband and words for her stepdaughter. Much of what she was saying didn't make much sense. She was far too distraught for making anything like logical sense but that didn't matter too much just then. She was making her own kind of sense, emotional sense.

She was a woman whose baby had been stolen from her and she wanted her baby back. She wanted him back at any cost and she didn't want anyone asking her to wait or to have patience. She wanted action. The people who had her baby wanted money and she was ready to give it to them. They could have all the money in the world. If it left her poor, what difference did that make? She'd been poor before. She could be poor again. Money wasn't anything.

"They're stalling," she sobbed. "Their own flesh and blood and they're stalling. Putting it off till Monday, putting it off two whole days till Monday. She did that. Miss Fixit did it. Her father's daughter with a head for business and a heart for nothing. They'll have to wait till Monday when the banks are open just like it was the grocery bill or Bergdorf's. She talks to them. She makes deals with them. She does it, not me. It isn't her baby. It's mine. I want my baby back."

"Gloria," her husband moaned. "It isn't the money. I told you a thousand times it isn't the money. Five hundred thousand dollars. Nobody carries money like that around in his pants pocket. I have to raise it and I can't before Monday. I told you that."

"You told me," she screamed. "You've both been telling me all night. I'm sick of your telling me. Telling me doesn't get me my baby back. And it's not like you don't know who's got him. You know all right. You both of you know and you think you've been fooling me. She's got him and she's not going to keep him, not till Monday even, not even till tomorrow. I'll kill her first."

"Gloria," Stewart growled. "Stop that. I don't want to hear another word of that. It's crazy and you're going to stop it."

"It's crazy and letting her have my baby isn't crazy? Sitting around on your ass and waiting till Monday isn't crazy? No matter what you do, that's sane. That's right. That's the correct thing to do like the correct people do it. The only thing that's crazy is for me even to say her name. Cheap, common me, I mustn't even talk about high and mighty her. She's too good for me even to talk about. Okay, Lon Stewart, to hell with that. To hell with you. To hell with the lot of you. I'll say it and say it and say it. Susan, old bitch Susan. Susan, Susan, Susan."

Stewart dropped into a chair and buried his head in his hands. His daughter, who had been standing white-faced and flinching under each word as though, word by word, they were cuts of a whip, went to him.

"Daddy," she said softly. "I'm sorry, Daddy. It's my

fault. I should have gone to her when you told me to. I should have tried to keep her quiet. It was just that I didn't think I could. I have tried, Daddy. You know I have. I'm sorry."

Three

It did, of course, take time; but eventually they'd simmered down enough so that they were talking to us again. That, however, didn't get us too much beyond where we'd been. Stewart and his daughter gave up on their valiant but feeble attempts at trying to make us believe there'd been no kidnaping. They had to come around that much. Mrs. Gloria Stewart had torn that for them; but, beyond the bare admission, they weren't ready to give us anything.

The only one of the family at all ready to trust us was Mrs. Gloria Stewart and she, unfortunately, was the one who had nothing to give but emotion. That she did give and unstintingly but, except for having supplied us with the first big break, she did us more harm than good. Stewart himself was determined to play it for recovery of the child and nothing else. He was going to raise the ransom and he was going to pay it. He wanted his baby back and he wanted nothing else.

If we'd had to cope with only him, we probably could have worked out some decent scheme of co-operation. He could have been convinced that we would make good on our promises. It wouldn't have been too difficult to make him believe that we would hold off and that we would hold the police off until every last possibility of co-operation with the kidnapers had been exhausted. We could also have convinced him that, even on a progam of following to the letter all instructions he would receive from the kidnapers, he could profit from our advice and help. He undoubtedly would have shied away from any suggestion that we put a tap on his telephone line, but I think we could have sold him even on that.

We could have done a lot if it hadn't been for the two women. Between his wife and his daughter that character was whipsawed. Gloria wanted action, quick action and lots of it. What she wanted was so crazy that anyone who wasn't at least as hysterical as she was would know right away that her notions could get her nothing but a dead baby.

Weighing in against her at every point we had Emily. Emily in her own way was equally hysterical. Emily wanted no part of us. She took no stock in any of our promises or assurances. Every step of the way she warned her father against us. Emily was in there hitting with the simplest possible approach. The kidnapers had Little Lonnie and to her that meant that they were holding the only stake that counted for anything. It was a game in which they had all the chips. They had control of the kid's safety. His life was in their hands.

She had received the ransom call. The kidnaper had

talked to her. She knew how much he was to be feared. She had to make them understand what a terrible mistake they would be making when they took even the slightest chance of angering the man. Little Lonnie might only be her half brother, but they knew how she felt about him. She loved him as much as they did and it wasn't even any use talking about that. He was a baby and she would feel the same about any baby. She was afraid, afraid for the baby, and every word they spoke to us was terrifying her. They shouldn't have told us anything. Just in telling us they had spoken Little Lonnie's death sentence. She waved away our promises, arguing that now the Stewarts could only hope we'd keep them.

"When nobody but us knew that Lonnie had been kidnaped," she said, "we knew nothing would be done for anything but Lonnie's safety."

"Believe me, Miss Stewart," I said, trying where Gibby had failed, "we're right with you there and the police will be, too. It would be monstrous if that wasn't the first and only consideration."

"And Dora," Bud Bronson growled. "What about Dora?"

"Dora and the baby, of course," I said.

"What's so of course?" Bronson demanded. "It's like I said. It's Dora you got to worry about. Who bothers to bump off a baby? A baby can't go fingering nobody. A baby can't go leading the cops to where he was held. You can get the baby back all right, but do we ever get to see Dora again?"

"If we don't get to see that girl again," Emily said, fighting her fear with anger, "it will be your fault because with your interference you've scared the kidnapers. If not that, it will be because she won't want to come back. With her share of half a million dollars she may have better places to go."

Bronson took a step forward and his hand came up. It was obvious that he had forgotten that he'd never hit a dame in his life, not even a dame who wasn't Dora. Emily watched him come at her and she never flinched. This was a girl with that kind of courage. She could be afraid for her baby brother, not for herself. When Gibby and I made grabs at him and shoved him away, she looked as though she couldn't have cared less, not even the smallest flash of relief or of gratitude. This was a babe with guts.

For all her panic, she also had confidence. The kidnaper had talked to her. She was the one who had been given the instructions. She had heard the man's voice. She knew how far he could be trusted. She knew what must be done and what must not be done. Just from talking to him on the telephone, she knew that this was no ordinary criminal. The man who had told her what must be done was a person of intelligence, a man of brains. She was ready to believe that he would be a man of his word as well.

"He's been smart enough to find out everything he needs to know about us," she said. "When he telephoned here, he picked his time and it was a time when neither Daddy nor Gloria was here. He called when he knew he would get me. That wasn't an accident. He wants to deal with me. He's been watching us and studying us. He's afraid of Daddy. Try as he might to follow instructions, Daddy could come to that moment when he'd do something brave and foolish. Any man would. If it was otherwise, he wouldn't be a man. He told me that. He said he was taking no chances and we weren't to take any. He had chosen to deal with me because he was counting on me to keep my head and be sensible."

"What else did he tell you aside from the flattery?" Gibby asked tartly.

"He told me it was up to me," she said. "He told me I'd have to keep Daddy from doing anything foolish and he told me Gloria would go hysterical and if I didn't watch her she would do something that could spoil everything. I can give it to you in his exact words. 'I'm no sadist,' he said. 'I like kids and I like people. I don't want to hurt anybody and I'm not going to hurt anybody unless I have to. I took the baby and I took the nurse, too. I took her because I had to have her. She knows how to feed him and how to take care of him and I don't. I could make a mistake and harm him without meaning to and I don't want to make any mistakes. You don't make any and you keep that dumb floosie your old man married from making any and nobody will get hurt. You'll have the kid back and he'll be as good as new.' Those were his exact words."

In quoting those exact words, she cast an apologetic look at her stepmother, emphasizing with the look that the words were the kidnaper's and not her own.

"So what's with cracks about Dora?" Bronson growled.

"He's had someone to tell him everything he needs to know about us," Emily said. "That could be Dora."

Gloria pushed her hair away from her face, making

even a worse mess of her mascara in the process. "I may be a dumb floosie," she wailed, "but I know what I know and I never forget anything. I haven't forgotten where that high-and-mighty Miss Bitch came from. I was crazy ever to let her go near my child."

There was a lot of that, back and forth, and we had to assume that they knew what they were talking about. The kidnaper had impressed Emily with his good sense, his ability to see right through the walls of the Stewart house and detect even the slightest wandering from the strictest letter of his instructions, his business acumen, and possibly even his integrity.

She regretted the fact that we had come to the house at all. She further regretted that we hadn't been gotten out of there without learning anything. Now she was desperately resolved that we be convinced that we must go away. We must keep hands off completely. We must leave her to deal with the kidnaper, without aid, without interference, without surveillance.

It was a fine exhibition of bravery and girlish spunk, but I think her father could have been shown the idiocy of going along on it without any help from us if Gloria had not been around to make all alternatives sound completely insane. Gloria was grasping at straws and when Gibby or I offered even the most moderate and careful of suggestions, Gloria would snatch at it and in her desperate enthusiasm she would turn it to straw.

There was the question of telephone contacts, for instance. Just on what Emily had told us of the first contact it was obvious that this man she was touting as an efficiency expert in the kidnaping field might well be prone to make one ridiculously simple mistake and it was a mistake that could be magnificently useful to us. On that first contact he had allowed himself to be far more garrulous than is ordinarily considered to be consonant with sound technique in kidnaping circles.

All he had to do on a future contact would be to permit himself to take the time on the telephone for talking as picturesquely, extensively, and in as elaborated detail as she had quoted to us and we could be in business. Tracing a call to its source is no great trick. It takes only a little time. You have the phone company alerted that you'll be wanting the job done. As soon as the call comes through and you know it's the one you want, you turn them loose on it. Given the amount of time it would take for such a speech as Emily had quoted to us, they'll have the originating point of the call.

After that all you need is that he use the same phone twice and you can be waiting for him. Even failing that, there are possibilities. You have the neighborhood marked and you can be ready. The next time he calls you'll have men spotted around the neighborhood and they can close in on him, even if he has been moving from phone to phone.

It's never sure-fire and mostly it's worth all too little, but mostly people who go in for kidnaping don't go in for talking at the length this bird had talked to Emily. That could be a habit, and if it was we had the most unusual possibilities. We tried to sketch those possibilities in for them. Emily was opposed to so much as thinking about them. Her father looked interested. Gloria picked up the idea and was off and running with it.

She would take the next call. The kidnaper would have to go all the way back to the beginning and start all over with her. That way she could keep him on the telephone just as long as we would want him. She did a full production job on it. She would hold him. We would close in on him and that would be it. We would bring her baby home again. There would be no waiting for Monday or for the banks or for any other nonsense.

"He won't talk to anyone but me," Emily said. "He was emphatic about that."

"That is just the kind of thing we can't do," Stewart said gently, making a try at explaining it to her.

It was explaining the obvious. He was telling her that even if they did have the police on it they would still have to make every effort to follow the kidnaper's instructions most exactly. The very fact that they might not really be doing exactly as he had told them would be an additional reason to keep the surface of the thing going most strictly according to the rules the man had laid down.

He wasted his breath. She never listened to a word of it. Even as he began to speak, she sensed that he was not falling in with this idea of hers. That was enough for her. It set her right off again into the old round of hysterical accusations. He didn't care about his child. He didn't want the baby back. Money was more important to him than was Little Lonnie. Her poor baby. Nobody cared about the poor little thing, nobody but his poor mother. His father was a monster, without heart or feelings.

It was she, of course, who had whipped up this idea

of getting the child back without putting out a penny of the ransom money. Her husband and her stepdaughter were holding out for giving the kidnaper everything he wanted up to and including the five hundred grand, but nothing could make her see it that way. For her there was nothing that necessarily followed on anything else. She'd been hurt and she was hitting back and she was in a state where words had no meaning for her beyond their capacity for hurting her or the possibility of her using them to hurt someone else. She was the one ally we had in the family but for my money we could have done better with our adversaries.

The real adversary, of course, was Emily. She was the gal who was holding the key cards and she wasn't letting anyone have so much as a peek at them. They had been dealt out to her by the kidnaper. He had done a terrific job of scaring her into playing them close to the chest, and she was playing them so close that just asking her a question was like putting your mitt down inside her bra.

What little they gave us in the way of the facts we had from her father, and even when he tried to draw from her some small bit of further information she wasn't letting him have any more than he already knew. He reached the place where he was asserting his right to know, but she would get the shakes again and say she was afraid to tell him. She'd beg him not to ask her and she'd quote the kidnaper at him. It was for his own good that he shouldn't know.

"He told me not to tell Gloria or even you anything more than was absolutely necessary," she said. "He told me that keeping secrets was something a person did better without anyone to help her. A secret is safe in inverse proportion to the number of people who know it. Two people keep a secret only half as well as one."

"Inverse proportion?" Gibby muttered. "Were those his words, Miss Stewart?"

She hesitated a moment, as though she were trying to decide whether she should answer even a question like that. Evidently she decided that we could be trusted with that much information because she did answer.

"No," she said. "Those were my words. He said that two people keep a secret only half as well as one, three people only a third as well."

That was too much for Bud Bronson. "Jeez," he snarled. "How long do we stand around doing fractions?"

I felt with him and for him.

"This is the big deal, Bud," I told him. "We're getting this thing narrowed down. We have to deal with a snatch artist who is also a philosopher."

"A goddamn amateur," Bud moaned, "a goddamn amateur who'll end up killing Dora and the kid and hisself. I been afraid of that all along. Pulling a snatch, it always looks good to the amateurs. There ain't no kind of caper anywhere that's easier to start and harder to finish. They get into it and then they don't know how to get out. So everybody's dead."

It was the wrong thing to say in the hearing of the child's mother. Even a better organized mother than Gloria Stewart had ever been would cave under that one. Gloria caved. She was overdue anyhow. Stewart picked her up in his arms and carried her out of the room. We had things quieter for a bit, but there wasn't much we could do with Emily.

She had talked with the man and she could tell us that he'd said nothing that wasn't calm, sensible, and well thought out. This was not a man who would panic or do anything foolish. We could count on that. If we were sincere in our protestations that our first thought was for the safety of the child and of Dora Mason, we would go away and forget we'd ever been in the house or ever been told anything.

"Just leave me alone," she said. "Let me deal with him. I'll have Lonnie back unharmed. I'll also have Dora back if she wants to come. I hate saying this about the girl, but I have been thinking that a man like that wouldn't have risked taking her unless he had known he wasn't taking the risks he seems to have taken. As this gentleman said, she is an adult. She could give you a description of the man who held her and of the place he took her. Doesn't it piece together? His knowing as much as he did about us and his taking Dora along with Lonnie. It does seem as though he must have some good reason for thinking he has nothing to fear from Dora."

"He'll bump her off," Bronson groaned. "They ain't never a better reason than that."

"Only if there's interference," Emily Stewart insisted. "He really convinced me of that. He told me he will give me instructions for the delivery of the money. I don't know yet where I'll have to go to take it to him but from what he did tell me I know that he has that part of it completely planned. You may think he's an amateur, but it's obvious to me that he didn't get himself into this before he had worked out every last detail of how he would get out of it."

"He told you he has it all worked out?" Gibby asked.

"He told me how he's going to do it," she said. "I'll bring the money to a place he will tell me. He'll take me to Lonnie and Dora and he'll lock the three of us up together. The room where he's going to lock us up will have a telephone in it but he will have had the service on that phone temporarily disconnected. There will be no way we can let anybody know where we are so they can come and get us out. We'll have to wait till the phone has again been put into service. He said it would be one or two days but that before he left me he'd tell me how soon I could get a call out. By then, of course, he'll be out of reach."

"And you're going to trust him?"

"Lonnie's my brother. Do I have any choice? That's a good plan he has and I don't see how it can possibly go wrong unless there's interference. Why would he harm me if there's no interference?"

"And you think he'll trust you?"

Bronson had his own question to add to that.

"Just because he's put the snatch on Dora," he growled, "you been saying she's maybe in it with him. So now he's going to let you see him and let you see the place he's keeping them, but you're different."

"I shall be seeing him only briefly," Emily said. "I can see no way he could get the money, be sure it was right, and deliver Lonnie and Dora without letting someone see him. He has to make contact some way. He didn't have to kidnap Dora. Also I can see another reason for

51

his choosing me for his contact. He's been studying us and he's chosen me as the one who won't lose her head. Also it's something more to make my father behave and to make him force Gloria to behave. If I am followed or there's any kind of interference, my father will lose both of us, his son and his daughter."

"He's willing to let you take that chance?" Gibby asked.

"I haven't told him any of that yet. He will have to let me. None of us has any choice."

"Did the kidnaper tell you when to expect his next contact?"

"Yes."

"When?"

"I'm not telling anyone that. I'll be going to this man with the money. I'll be putting myself into his hands. He already has my baby brother. Do you think I would dare go if there was any chance that you'd be following me or if anything had been done that could give him even the slightest suspicion that we were not playing along with him completely? I'm not that brave."

I had to admire the girl's courage. That she was terrified was obvious. She was sick with fear. Her every nerve was standing on end and screaming, but she was like a man who was going into battle. She had faced up to what she thought she was going to have to do and somewhere she had found inside herself the steel she was going to need for doing it. That guy had done a job on her over the phone. He'd convinced her that she was going to have to deal with him. It would have to be Emily Stewart and no one else. Otherwise there would be no deal. He would dispose of the child and Dora and he would take off. She wasn't kidding herself. She knew the danger, but she had braced herself and she was ready to meet that danger. It was the thought of adding to the risk—and that was the way she was seeing it, as added risk—that made her go to pieces. She could bring herself up to carrying out this man's instructions. She couldn't face going into it carrying the knowledge that even to the slightest degree one of his orders had been disobeyed. That was the worst of her fears, the fear that something would be done and somehow he would know.

Her father came back into the room. "I brought her around," he said. "I persuaded her to take some phenobarb and lie down."

"You'd do better having a doctor for her," I advised.

Emily shuddered. "And more people knowing," she said, "and less chance of this coming out all right."

"She's resting now," Stewart said feebly.

We went to work on him and sweating it out bit by bit, we did get him to tell us what little he knew. It was done over his daughter's entreaties every step of the way, and each time he turned to her for corroboration or amplification he ran into the same stricken silence. She just begged him not to ask her and not to tell us any more. Her fear of crossing this kidnaper was something you couldn't reach with reasoning. It was like a superstitious terror.

What we got from Stewart was ordinary enough once you've recognized that kidnaping is such an extraordinary thing in anyone's life that even its most routine maneuvers

53

can hardly seem really ordinary. Stewart and his wife had been out to a cocktail party.

"We were going to the theater tonight and we were to come home to dress before the theater," he explained. "Emily had a date with a boy. She was home getting herself ready for her date and she was here alone except for Mary, the cook. Mary always goes up to her room for a nap in the afternoon and, since none of us was going to be here for dinner tonight and she had nothing to prepare for that, she hadn't come down. When the phone rang, Emily answered it."

It had been the kidnaper calling. Gibby interrupted to ask the exact time. Stewart referred to Emily. She begged him not to ask her. She begged him to stop talking.

"It was some time before five-thirty," Stewart told us after he'd given up on trying to persuade his daughter to let us have even that paltry bit of exact information. "It was five-thirty when Emily got me at the cocktail party. She said I had to come home to her right away. She needed me."

That was some babe, that Emily. Right from the very first she'd been taking no chances. Her father had asked what she wanted him for and she'd said she needed him. Wasn't that enough? He'd told her to be reasonable and she said she was being reasonable. She was in a jam and she needed him right away. She told him to say she was sick and he had to go to her but to come at once.

As he told it, he'd tried to go home alone but Gloria had been too much concerned for her stepdaughter to stay on at the party without him. That part of it had a pretty phony ring to it but in any event Gloria had come home with him.

Emily had been waiting for them and she had been ready to roll. Evidently it had not occurred to this kidnaper who, according to her, was a character who thought of everything, that late on a Saturday afternoon might be a bad time for setting up a cash transaction of half a million dollars.

Evidently it hadn't occurred to Emily either, but after all she must have been pretty much in shock and if there was anything astonishing about her it was that she had been able to think as clearly as she did about any of it. The kidnaper wasn't in shock. He had made himself a complete plan, but still he had expected that Hulon Stewart could get all that cash up for him on demand, that there wouldn't be even the briefest of natural delays.

That may seem like the craziest kind of ignorance to you or to me, but thinking about it, I came to the conclusion that for a kidnaper who, on the basis of Bud Bronson's quick researches, appeared to be not one of the regulars in that profession, it might very well figure. As for Emily, even without shock she might not have known. Gloria was still unable to understand the delay.

Emily, after all, was a rich man's daughter. Any time she'd wanted dough, she probably had asked Daddy and Daddy had never failed to dig down into his pants and come up with the desired sum. Daddy had probably not come up with the actual cash. I could guess that he'd written a check or he'd told her it would be okay for her to go out and have whatever it was she wanted charged

55

to him. That, however, was a difference that was not likely to have impressed Emily.

In one form or another it had been money. One of Daddy's checks had always been as good as cash and there had never been the least thing wrong with Daddy's credit. The checkbook and the Diner's Club card had merely been cleaner and more convenient to handle than great wads of dirty currency and either had always produced currency any time of the day or night and any day of the week she had wanted it. It just hadn't entered her head that this would be different.

It should have entered the kidnaper's head and the very fact that it hadn't did make it seem as though Bud Bronson had hit it on the nose when he'd concluded his Dora and Little Lonnie Stewart were in the hands of an amateur. People who aren't very rich and who haven't had any occasion to look closely into the habits of the very rich are prone to assume that the very rich are always surrounded by money. That's a mistake. Ask an experienced burglar or a well-seasoned holdup man. They'll tell you. They know that the best victim is the gent who's comfortably well off or just a little bit rich. He'll have cash on him and he'll have cash around the house. He'll also have available his wife's jewelry.

Get into the upper brackets and you don't do nearly as well. Credit comes too easily up there. Your real Croesus doesn't carry money on him. It spoils the hang of his suit. As for his wife's jewelry—there'll be so much of it that, except for special occasions, it's always tucked away in a bank vault.

It was obvious that Hulon Stewart was very rich. He

was squawking some at the prospect of raising half a million bucks but he was obviously confident that, once the banks were open, he would be able to raise it and quickly. The difficulty is that he just doesn't have anything like five hundred thousand dollars in any of his pockets. He can comb out every pocket he owns and Gloria and Emily can upend their purses and among the three of them they aren't going to be able to get up even one thousand.

It's at that point, of course, that the trouble starts with Gloria. He should have had the dough on hand. What's the good of having money when you can't lay your hands on it at a time when you need it and most particularly at a time like this, when you need it so desperately? There's always been money for everything else, but not now when the life and safety of his baby son depend on it.

Both the women are upset, but Emily is still keeping her head. She's the one who comes up with the suggestion that he try a couple of his friends. Can't he borrow a hundred thousand here and a hundred thousand there? Stewart knows better. His friends aren't gangsters or racketeers. They don't keep large sums in cash around for emergencies any more than he does. They're respectable men. They don't have five-hundred-grand emergencies on Saturday afternoons. He didn't give us any sort of detail on what his wife thought about that sort of respectability, but you can make your own guess on that.

So Emily says they don't have to wait for the banks to open. They have friends who are bankers. Daddy can call on his friends. Any one of them will be happy to open his bank up specially at a time like this. So then he has to explain about bank vaults and time clocks and

57

Emily, disappointed as she is, does, nevertheless, understand. By then, of course, he has triggered Gloria's third-stage rocket. She's way up there and no bringing her down. She doesn't believe a word of it. He's only making excuses. He's thinking more of the money than he is of her baby.

He tries to reason with her and Emily tries to reason with her but they get nowhere and after about an hour of this Emily has to take off. It's time for her second contact with the kidnaper.

Gibby did try to persuade her to give us her account of that but by this time she is paralyzed with terror and every word Stewart is letting us have scares her more. She's just about scared speechless.

Except for riding along on the advice she'd had in that initial contact with the kidnaper, she's paralyzed. She can beg Daddy to stop talking to us but that's all. The safety of a secret is in inverse proportion to the number of people who know it. From the first she had known that it would be safest if she took no one into her confidence. She'd had no choice. She'd had to tell her father since he was the one who would have to get up the money, but she hadn't wanted to tell Gloria. It would have been so much better all around if it had gone the way she had wanted it to go. Gloria would have stayed on at the cocktail party. Her father would have come home alone. He would have gotten the five hundred thousand up immediately. She would have had her second contact with the kidnaper and she would have been able to tell him that she had the money and was ready to pay it over. He would have told her where to take it. She would have had Dora and the baby back home before Gloria would even have known that they'd been gone and before Bronson would have come around to spend the evening.

"You're forgetting," Gibby told her, "that when you do deliver the ransom you're going to be left with Dora and the child in a locked room with a dead telephone and that it will be a day or two before service is restored on that line so you can phone out and tell your father where he can come and get you."

If you think Gibby was forgetting that Stewart had been out of the room when she'd told us that or that Gibby didn't remember that she'd said she hadn't told her father that part of it yet, you just don't know Gibby. He wasn't forgetting anything. He was dropping that into the hopper in full deliberation. If anything could slip a wedge between father and daughter, that could have been expected to do it.

It did produce a crisis. Stewart flipped. Emily flipped. Stewart said we were crazy if we thought he'd ever hold still for any arrangement like that. Emily said that it just went to show that she was completely right. We weren't to be trusted. We couldn't keep our great flapping mouths shut about anything. She turned to her father and begged him to be reasonable. There was no question of what he'd hold still for and what he wouldn't hold still for. The kidnaper had Lonnie and, as long as the baby was in that man's hands, they would have to do exactly as the man said. They had to do it if they were ever to be able to live with themselves again. She wasn't afraid to go and there was no reason for her father to be afraid of letting her go. Only one thing could put her in danger and that

59

would be if they even seemed to be talking to the police, if they even seemed to be disregarding the kidnaper's instructions in so much as the smallest and most trifling detail.

They went round and round about that and came to no conclusions, but it was easy to see that Emily would prevail. Her father didn't like any of it but she had the clincher and she kept throwing it at him. It didn't matter whether they liked it or not. They had no choice, not if he wanted Little Lonnie back.

He did tell us about the second contact, though. The kidnaper had picked Emily as the one member of the family who would keep her head. He had set it up to deal with Emily and with no one but Emily. He'd made his first call to the house at a time when neither Stewart nor Gloria would be home. For the second contact he'd told Emily to leave the house and go to a designated telephone booth. She was to wait there till a call came in. She'd gone out to wait for the call and she'd begged her father and Gloria to let her go alone and not to ask her where the booth was or what time she was to be there waiting for the call. The kidnaper had specifically warned her against telling anyone. She'd be too frightened even to speak to him if she'd made so much as the smallest departure from the road he had laid down for her.

So she goes out for the contact. She's gone more than a half hour. She comes back and reports. Lonnie is all right. He's had his bottle and he's sleeping. The kidnaper has given her an exact description of the position in which the kid slept and no one could do that unless he'd seen Lonnie fall asleep.

She's told the kidnaper how much Daddy thought he could raise in cash without waiting for the banks to open and she's asked him if he won't give them a break and take that. Stewart has made a try at raising some cash. He's tried all his clubs. They keep funds on hand for cashing checks and he's asked each one how large a check they could handle for him. He's also called around to friends and asked them what they could manage out of what they might have on hand in their wall safes. He's rounded up promises that added to so close to a hundred thousand that he's certain he could find enough more to make the round sum. She's offered the kidnaper that, an immediate hundred grand.

The kidnaper is not happy about waiting till Monday but he's not settling for twenty cents on the dollar. So Emily has to make him understand about banks and time clocks and about how the Stewarts use checks and credit so much that they have hardly any cash at all available. He agrees to wait until Monday and he tells her to come out and make contact again after the banks are open Monday and after Daddy has the money ready to hand over. He's set a Monday time when he would call her.

"Emily knew we'd go crazy waiting till Monday and knowing nothing," Stewart said. "She persuaded him to call her before then. He will be in touch periodically tonight and tomorrow and tomorrow night. We'll have reports on how the boy is."

And there we were. That was everything he knew and it was all we were getting. Emily hadn't told him when or where she would be going for her next contact. He didn't even know whether she had been given a schedule of the promised contacts or whether each call was setting up the next.

"I'm just hoping he will make the next call," Emily said, speaking out of what sounded like total misery. "If he's having us watched, it may be all finished by now. He told me I'm being watched when I go out for the calls. If I'm not alone, if there's any interference, that will be the end of it. We'll never hear from him again."

"The usual threat," Gibby said.

"There have been cases of kidnaped babies that have been murdered," Stewart groaned. "Since Emily has the courage to carry on, I'm going to let Emily do it. I have no choice. You must keep hands off, gentlemen. You must."

"She'll go alone," Gibby promised. "We won't follow her and we won't have her followed. Who's Susan?"

The quick switch caught Stewart off stride. He colored and winced.

"Oh, that," he said hurriedly. "You must disregard anything my wife says. She's hysterical. You can understand that certainly. A mother . . ."

"All that about Susan," Emily said, "will show you just how hysterical Gloria is. Susan is my mother."

I looked at the girl and I understood how her father had been able to force himself to the decision to let her carry through on this. The girl had it. She was eaten hollow with terror and grief and humiliation. I had seen the way she looked when Gloria had been whipping her with her mother's name. Now I couldn't even begin to estimate what it had cost this girl to say those few words. Somehow she had found the means. She had said them. There was nothing Emily Stewart had to do that she couldn't do. I wanted to bow to her.

Four

So there we were. Stewart had been a long time making up his mind, but, once he'd done it, there was no more moving him. We were to keep hands off. He was letting Emily see it through. Gibby fought it all the way down the line but all he managed to achieve was one small concession. He wanted to set up a meeting between Stewart and the Old Man. That shouldn't have been too difficult, but Emily was desperately afraid of it and that made it rough.

She was certain that the house was being watched. She insisted that they could only hope that our having been there hadn't already ruined the whole deal.

"If these men keep coming in and out of the house," she said, "if they bring the District Attorney here, that will be the end. We're not dealing with a fool, Daddy. He'll know. The New York District Attorney is not just some nobody. He's a conspicuous figure. If he comes here, he'll be recognized. It's just what we can't risk."

64

"He doesn't have to come here," Gibby told her.

"My father goes to him? That's almost worse. My father walks out of this house and goes down to the District Attorney's office? What's that going to look like? A cocktail party?"

"The DA belongs to a lot of clubs," Gibby said. "University Club, New York Athletic, Union League. If none of those will do, Mr. Stewart, name any one of your clubs and I'll fix it for him to drop in there. I'm sure Miss Stewart could explain your going to one of your clubs. Satisfying the kidnaper on that won't take too much doing. Miss Stewart has already told him you asked at your clubs and you hit your friends and you can give him a hundred thousand tonight. You go to one of your clubs. What could be more natural? It can even be used to show the kidnaper you're still trying. You don't want to keep him waiting until Monday."

"The Union League," Stewart said. "I'm a member. The University Club, too, but the Union League will be better. There's more money at the Union League."

"I'll set it up," Gibby said, getting in there quickly. "I'll get after the DA right away. You hold yourself available and I'll let you know the time by telephone."

"I'll be available," Stewart promised.

Emily threw herself on his neck. "Daddy," she sobbed. "You're crazy. No matter how it's done, you can't be sure it's safe. How do we know the phone isn't tapped? You can be followed to the club and watched. The District Attorney is seen going in. These people aren't stupid. You can't do it, Daddy."

I could see him waver.

65

"Maybe," he began and he was looking for the words with which he could back down.

We weren't waiting for them. "It'll be safe," I argued. "We won't call here at all. We'll pick a good name. Make it a money-sounding name. How's Pierrepont? You call the Union League and ask if Mr. Pierrepont is in the club. Leave word for them to call you any time Mr. Pierrepont comes in. Then you'll get the call from there. Somebody on the club staff will make it."

"Daddy," Emily said. "You call the Union League and ask if Mr. Pierrepont has come in. They'll ask what Mr. Pierrepont. They'll say they have no Mr. Pierrepont. The whole club staff will have to be in on it. You can't do it, Daddy. It's too many people."

Stewart hauled out his handkerchief and mopped his face. "Emily's right," he said. "We can't risk it."

"All right," Gibby conceded. "That's too fancy. I have a better way. It's simpler. You go to the Union League tomorrow morning. Ten o'clock, that's as early as could look reasonable. Go there then. If for any reason the DA can't make it then, there will be word for you giving you the time. You come back when it's time. That will look all right. You went there to see if you could raise some money without waiting till Monday for the banks. You weren't successful. You try again later. That's all right."

"What's all right about going to the Union League at ten on Sunday morning?" Emily wailed. "Who goes there then? It will look crazy. You want him to go out of his way to behave suspiciously."

This time Stewart answered her. We had won a point. "No, dear," Stewart said. "That will be all right. It is early and it is the weekend but, even if they do watch me, that will be all right. I can look that anxious."

"But why take the chance, Daddy? You can't let them interfere, no matter what. What can you talk to the District Attorney about? It's so completely pointless."

"I can think of one thing there might be a lot of point in talking about," Gibby said. "Some way will have to be worked out for satisfying our friend Bronson here and for keeping him quiet. I can think of ways but we don't have the authority for it. That would have to come through the Old Man."

"I ain't keeping quiet for nobody," Bronson growled. "They got Dora and I ain't keeping quiet for nobody."

"See what I mean?" Gibby murmured. "Bronson can go to the police. He can go to the newspapers. You can't go it alone. There's no way you can control Bronson."

"They's no way nobody can control me," Bronson snarled.

"Keep your shirt on, Bud," Gibby told him. "We're all after the same thing. This guy has Dora. You don't want anything scaring him into doing something he doesn't have to do."

Bronson wasn't too certain. "You keep that in front of you," he said sullenly. "You keep that in front of you all the time. This creep, he ain't only got the kid. He's got Dora, too, and they better both be coming back safe or I'll be wanting to know why."

"I can tell you why right now," Emily sobbed. "It will be because you couldn't mind your own business. You had to interfere."

The words flew back and forth between the two of

them and that was doing no good. We hauled Bronson out of there, but at the cost of stirring him up we'd accomplished our purpose. We left with Hulon Stewart's promise. He would be at the Union League Club at ten in the morning. It didn't seem good having to wait for it but we did have that. We'd have the Old Man there to back us up, and we'd have a chance at Stewart without the women.

Once we were outside the house, of course, Bronson turned on us.

"I ain't holding still for none of this," he announced.

Gibby winked at him. "Look, Bud," he said. "You think we're smart, don't you?"

"You're too goddamned smart. It's like I knew it was going to be. Everybody's thinking about the baby and to hell with what's happening to Dora."

"We're thinking about Dora," Gibby said.

"You ain't doing nothing."

"There's nothing anybody can do till Emily gives us something to go along on. She's so scared we can't get anything out of her. We're setting it up to talk to Stewart alone. That's our only chance. We have to get it out of him. We get him alone and we get him to make some sense. Till then we have to lie low."

Bronson didn't like it. "Leave me have a half hour alone with that Emily babe," he said grimly. "I'll get it out of her all right."

Gibby groaned. "Now why didn't we think of that?" he said. "Such a good idea and so simple. We turn you loose on her. You beat the daylights out of her and what do you get? You get everything she knows like which phone booth she goes to when she waits for the kidnaper to call her. Of course, she's in no shape to go there and do a cool-headed job of talking to him. He panics. He kills the baby. He kills Dora. He takes off, but that's all right. We've got all we want. We've got a phone booth. What'll you do with the phone booth then, Bud? Stuff it?"

"All right," Bronson growled. "So you're smart. So you got better ideas?"

"No ideas at all are better than that," Gibby said, "but we've got better ideas."

"Like what?"

"Like going back to our place, getting on the telephone, filling the DA in on this thing and starting things moving on some kind of official basis."

"That's an idea for keeping your nose clean," Bronson said. "What does it get Dora?"

"Come along and see."

Gibby flagged down a cab. He held the door open for Bronson to get in. Bud hung back.

"Okay," I said. "Move it. We've got to get going."

"You get going," Bronson said. "I'll be seeing you."

"Where are you off to?" Gibby asked him.

"I can ask around some more," Bronson said. "I know people."

"All the times we had you brought in you never knew anybody."

"Then it was different."

"Maybe," Gibby said. "But there's this one thing you don't want to forget. Emily has some good common sense on her side, and you said it yourself. If this is some amateur creep we're dealing with, it can be lucky that he's a creep who's figured he has a good way out of what he's got himself into. Our best bet for getting Dora back the way you want her is if nothing starts him thinking that maybe his way out won't work as well as he thought it would."

"I'll be careful," Bronson said. "I'll be careful, and I'll be in touch."

"How careful?"

"Careful."

"Let the cops in on it," Gibby warned, "and you'll have prowl cars with sirens howling. They'll be filling the street in front of the Stewart house and the kidnaper will notice that. Not good for Dora."

"I know."

"You're not going to forget?"

"Look," Bronson said. "When did I ever let no cops in on anything?"

"You're a changed man," I said. "When did you let us in on anything?"

"I hope I ain't made a mistake," Bronson growled. "With cops I know I'd be making a mistake."

"With newspapers, too," Gibby said.

"Newspaper," Bronson snarled. He took time out to spit, clearing the taste of the word out of his mouth. "From newspapers nobody ever had no break. I ain't no dope, man. I know how it's got to be. Quiet and quick. For Dora it's got to be quiet and quick."

"These people you're going to ask," Gibby said. "Will they know that it has to be quiet and quick?"

"Where I'm going to ask," Bronson said, "they don't

70

never talk to nobody, least of all cops or newspapers."

He took off. I started to climb into the cab but Gibby yanked me out of it and told the cabby we wouldn't be wanting him. The cabby didn't like it but we walked away from that. We pulled over to Third where we hit a bar and grill that had phone booths. We took a booth apiece and we both worked the phones. I called the Old Man. He didn't like being hauled out of bed, but even the bare bones of a report that I fed him over the phone took care of that. He wanted us up at his place right away. He'd be waiting for us.

I hung up and opened the door to Gibby's booth to give him the news.

"We see the Old Man in his pajamas," I said. "We've got to move or he'll catch a chill."

"We'll move," Gibby said and pushed the door shut.

It was for only a minute or two, though, and then he came out and we got rolling. I asked him whom he had called.

"The department," he said. "Who else? Something just might leak to them about this. I didn't want them making any calls to the Stewart place or sending any squad cars around there without checking in with us first. They're putting the word out and we'll have every cop in town keeping an eye out for Bronson. Once somebody spots him, he's going to be tailed."

"What for?"

"Just in case he was too much disappointed in us to keep in touch. The entry we've got into this deal is far too good to let anything queer it now."

"You counting that much on the meeting with Stewart in the morning?"

"Are you?"

"It's like you told Bronson. The best we'll get out of that is a phone booth and if I'm reading that babe Emily right, with the scare this kidnaper's thrown into her we won't get even that."

"You're reading her right. She gets more scared all the time. Not less. We've got everything now we'll ever get from her and with a little luck it can be enough."

I thought about that awhile. "The phone out of service gimmick," I said. "Something we can do with that?"

"There has to be something we can do with it. If Emily would co-operate, we could fix it to tail her when she goes to pay over the ransom."

"She won't co-operate. I can tell you that now."

"I've been telling myself," Gibby muttered.

At that point we flagged us a cab and that put a lid on any talk. The size cabs come in New York these days, you have the hackie sitting in your lap. You can't swap any ideas about tails and ransom payments under those conditions. There isn't much of anything you can do except think. I worked on doing that.

It was a cute little problem. You have the co-operation of the family of the kidnap victim. You work things out to take the absolutely irreducible minimum of risk. That's the best you can do. When it's kidnaping, there's no such thing as working it out so there will be no risk at all. Everybody is skillful. Nobody goofs. Everybody's nerves hold steady. You get your share of luck. If you have all that, you have a decent chance of bringing something off, but you don't have any more than that, only a decent chance.

In these things you always have to be weighing against that decent chance the other thing. There's always the indecent chance that somewhere along the line at any of a million little points something is going to go out of whack and you bring off nothing but a disaster. Nobody wants to come out of a thing like this with nothing to show for it but a dead baby. Even if you have an ideal setup and that means a family that's come to you for help, a family that's been convinced all the way that, however they come out of it with you, they couldn't come out better without you, even then you've failed and show me a failure anywhere in the law enforcement business that's more miserable than that one.

We didn't have anything like the ideal setup. I could see no hope that by Monday morning we could have Emily talked around to where she would be working with us. If we tailed her, it would have to be without her knowledge and probably without her father's knowledge as well. Do that and something goes wrong and then where are you? You've got it, boy. You're way up there without a paddle. You were asked to go away and keep your mitts off it, but you interfered. Why didn't you go in there and kill the baby yourself? What you've done amounts to much the same thing.

I tried it another way. We bring off a miracle. We get Hulon Stewart alone and we get him to take a sensible view. He goes home and he sells Emily on it. We do have co-operation. That's a pipe dream, but I'm trying all the possibilities on for size. Is the miracle any good to us? Taking a hard look at it, I'm forced to the conclusion that it isn't any good at all, which may sound like sour grapes. It isn't sour grapes. It's sound judgment.

The greatest asset I can find in the whole grim picture is Emily Stewart's almost mystical confidence in her dealings with this kidnaper. The babe believes in herself. She believes in this lug who's snatched her baby brother. Half brother? All right, but isn't half enough? The babe has a lovely, rich disdain for the trifling sum of five hundred thousand dollars. She's ready to go wherever she's told and swap the five hundred grand for Little Lonnie and, even scared as she is, she'll do it and she'll bring it off if anyone can. She won't make any mistakes.

A babe like Emily can have a beautifully soothing effect on even the most nervous of kidnapers, but let us not kid ourselves. There is the one necessary base for this dame's confidence and competence. It is her firm belief that all she has to do is play it straight with the kidnaper and he'll play it straight with her. Let her go to him with nothing on her conscience and she's got an excellent chance of bringing it off. Send her to him with the knowledge that she's double-crossing the bastard and the odds are at least a hundred to one that Emily will come apart. The more I thought about it, the less I found myself wishing for a co-operative Emily. A co-operative Emily would be a collapsed Emily. I was ready to take bets on that. Let her know she had somebody tailing her and she'd be no good to anybody.

"It has to be a phone that's been temporarily disconnected," I said, choosing words that would be okay for the hackie's big ears. "The instrument has to be there and the wiring has to be there. It can't be anything that requires a service man going around to do anything or even to make a check."

"People do it all the time," Gibby said, "when they lock up a house and go away awhile. It makes for a big saving on the phone bill; but you still have the installation intact and when you want service restored, you can have it without waiting."

"Sure," I said. "It's the sensible thing to do."

"And," Gibby added, "he's a sensible man with a sharp eye for a buck. That's certainly Emily's impression of him."

"But," I said, thinking aloud, "it doesn't seem likely that the company would bother doing it for a day or two and anyhow I can't see how anybody could go about explaining to the phone company wanting phone service off for twenty-four or forty-eight hours."

It could have been wonderfully easy for us that way. This was October, not one of the peak vacation months for people living in New York, but nevertheless I was guessing that the telephone company would be having a great many of these temporary suspensions of service. It would run to hundreds at least, if not into the thousands. Checking out any list, however long, is no impossibility. It can be done. It just takes time and patience and, although we could find the patience for it if we had to, we were not going to have the time. We had only until Monday.

If, however, we could find a request for a twenty-four-hour or forty-eight-hour suspension of service, we would be in. There could hardly be many of those at any time

and certainly there would be damn few for any one par-
ticular day. A request to have a phone temporarily disconnected for twenty-four or forty-eight hours beginning
Monday would certainly put us into business. I was going to be very much astonished if the phone company
came up with more than one of those and, if they came
up with more than the merest handful, I was just not
going to believe it. It seemed too easy. We could have the
search narrowed down to one or two spots, or at worst to
no more than we could find men to cover. It was too
easy.

The hackie, as hackies will (particularly now that they
have been brought into such embarrassing proximity to
their passengers), made his contribution to the conversation.

"Nobody does it for a day or two," he said. "You can't
save enough dough on it to be worth the bothering and
anyhow the phone company won't do it. They got a minimum time, two weeks. Every year I go on vacation I do
it. I take two weeks always and the phone's disconnected
always. A couple of years ago we went away like always.
We get the phone off like always. Ten days we're gone
and we get a call. It's the wife's mother. She's sick. Ap-
pendicitis it was and we got to come back right away
because she's having the operation. You know how it
goes. We get home. I go down to the corner and give
the company a call. I tell them we come back early and
as how it's an emergency and all that so we want the
phone back in. No dice. It's got to be the two weeks. It
can't be less. The only way I got it back on right off

was we forgot the whole deal and I paid the bill like it was on all the time."

We had the last of that after he'd pulled up and while I was paying him off. By the time he was out of earshot I had digested his bit of information. Maybe this could be easier than I'd thought.

"If that cabbie's right," I said to Gibby, "we may be able to set up a really good deal with the phone company. Suppose this bird doesn't know that it has to be a minimum of two weeks. He calls Monday morning and asks for a suspension of service for a day or two. We have them alerted for a call like that and I think we can get them to play along on giving him what he asks for. We can have him surrounded when Emily goes to pay the ransom. We pick him up complete with ransom after he's locked Emily and Dora and the kid up. We get him on his way out. There's not going to be more than one call like that Monday morning."

"If there's any call like that at all," Gibby said. "Anybody any time can pick up a phone, get the business office and ask for information on how to go about having a phone temporarily disconnected. He doesn't have to give his name and he can make the call from a phone booth anywhere. Nothing can be traced to him. There's too much planning gone into this, Mac, and too much research. This phone trick is too central to his getaway plan. He won't have left that to be done at the last minute without having checked it beforehand. We may have a couple of possibilities, but that's not one of them."

We'd been waiting for the elevator and at that point it came. The operator had obviously been sleeping down

77

in the basement and, even though he still had his eyes less than half open, it seemed a good idea not to say anything that would wake him up. I held it till we were upstairs and out of the elevator and then there was only the barest moment before the Old Man opened his apartment door to us.

I took that moment to unload a really discouraging thought that had slipped in on me during those few moments it had taken us to ride up from the lobby.

"We don't even know that it's a local phone," I said gloomily. "We have no way of knowing just what time the snatch was made. It could have been any time after Dora left the house with Lonnie, and we have only an approximation of the time Emily received the first call. There could be a spread of a couple of hours there, more than enough time to have taken them almost anywhere."

"That's been eating on me," Gibby said, "particularly since a room in which they can be locked for a day or two and no way of raising an alarm till phone service starts sounds like something in an isolated house. It doesn't sound like city stuff."

The Old Man took us out to the kitchen. He'd made himself a big pot of coffee to wake up on while he was waiting for us. He poured some out for us. This was something the voters of New York County hadn't considered when they voted the guy into the District Attorney's office. They'd elected a man who made horrible coffee. Even he himself didn't enjoy it. He was taking it down like medicine. I tasted mine and left it alone. I had enough bitterness to chew on without it.

We did a quick job of filling him in on everything we

had. Since you know how much that was, you can understand how it could be a really quick job. He approved the way we'd handled it as far as we'd been able to do any handling. He had one small criticism and that one was a switch. You have to know that the Old Man is rather especially fond of Gibby and he genuinely admires Gibby's dash and brilliance but he's always worried about the boy. He's always afraid Gibby will go too far and he's always in there telling me that the main part of my job is to keep a brake on Assistant DA Jeremiah X. Gibson just so he won't do anything too impulsive. The Old Man likes to keep things legal.

Now he was regretting that we hadn't been impulsive enough. "Bronson," he said. "I'm sorry you let go of him. If we had him locked up, we'd have a little better control of things."

"Obviously," Gibby agreed.

"But you didn't think of it?"

"We thought of it," Gibby said. "We thought of it longingly, but I decided we weren't in any position to push him around."

"With a record like his," the Old Man barked, "we're always in position. He's picked up for questioning."

That was the switch. He was actually quoting Gibby at Gibby.

"Hold it a second, sir," Gibby said. "Not for questioning. Whatever his record, he's reported a kidnaping to us. He's come to us with information and the information has checked out. You know how this thing ends, sir. The Stewarts get their kid back or they don't. Whichever way it goes, there will come that point where there's

79

no keeping this quiet any more and then the newspapers and the taxpayers will start asking how we handled ourselves. They're always accusing us of it even when we haven't done it—harassing babies with records for no reason except that they do have records. The Stewarts didn't ask us in on this. We pushed in. If anything goes wrong, it's automatically going to be our fault. This is a time when we have to worry about keeping our noses clean. We'll need the cleanest noses in town. The taxpayers are going to be looking at us."

You may not know it but when you're talking to an elected official taxpayers is the polite word to use. Voters is much too pointed. We always watch that when we're talking to the Old Man. We say taxpayers. We can leave it for the Old Man to translate the word to voters. He translated and the word worked its magic.

"I dare say you're right," the Old Man said with a sigh.

"Also," Gibby said, "I've talked to the department. The police will be catching up with Bronson and they'll be trailing him. That way he'll lead us to some of his contacts. That can be useful. Throw him in the can or let him know that we have him under surveillance, and he'll lead us to nothing."

"Not even to save this girl of his?" the Old Man asked.

"It would make him stop believing that we were trying to save his girl," I offered.

"I see what you mean," the Old Man said, accepting the inevitable.

"You'll meet Stewart tomorrow morning?" Gibby asked.

"Ten at the Union League, certainly. I'll want the two of you on hand for it."

"We carry on with this?"

"You haven't anything else to do."

"We carry on. Our best bet is that telephone gimmick."

Between us we'd knocked that one down pretty thoroughly even in the few minutes we'd had, and now Gibby was offering it as though it were something that was just oozing promise.

"A company list of temporarily disconnected telephones?" the Old Man groaned. "We don't have enough people even to begin a rundown on any list as long as that one is going to be."

"We have to give it the old try, sir," Gibby insisted.

The Old Man likes phrases like the "old try." They give him confidence. It isn't often that Gibby remembers that in talking to the Old Man it's a good idea to use those phrases. This was one night when he was remembering. There was a phone extension out there in the kitchen and Gibby used it. The Old Man's wife is one of those dames who like nice things. It was a pink telephone and I'd never seen Gibby with a pink telephone before. On him it didn't look right, but he wasn't noticing.

Telephones, of course, work a twenty-four-hour day and a seven-day week but that's for the ordinary business of putting calls through. For anything as special as what we wanted you do better if you can hit them during normal office hours and not on the weekend. It's not that they won't give the DA's office full co-operation any day or any time of day. It's just that at almost three o'clock of a Sunday morning they don't have any extra squads of people on hand who can hop right to it and whip out a special job of work for you. That's obvious. You can't expect that of any outfit.

Gibby worked at it and he got what he could. Our hackie had been very close to right. Their minimum period for a temporarily disconnected deal was fifteen days. He'd come within one day of that. They liked to have at least a day's notice for resumption of service. If anyone called in to ask for a suspension of a day or two, there would be no record of it. It would have been explained to him that there was the minimum period. If he took it for the fifteen days, it would appear in the records as that, with no mention that he had wanted it for the shorter period. If he had not taken it at all, there would be no record at all since there would be no action required.

All business office personnel who handled such calls could and would be alerted to record any requests for such a short-term suspension—a day or two or anything less than the fifteen—as might come in from then on and information on such calls would be relayed to us immediately. So much of it was relatively easy.

Then Gibby got on to the subject of the phones now temporarily disconnected.

"We're looking for a phone now out of service but which on your fifteen-day basis could have service resumed as early as tomorrow or the next day," he explained.

It was obvious that they were telling him how very many of those they had.

"Thousands," he said. "Of course, it would be that. Could you let our people work on the records? We'd want them to start with the most recent ones and work back. It will be a needle-in-the-haystack deal, of course, but we'll have to try it and we always can get lucky."

Gibby got it set up for what it was worth and, just on hearing his end of the conversation, we could gather that the telephone people didn't think it was worth much. He had one more request and one more question. The request reminded me of something I'd let slip my mind. He had told me that there were a couple of possibilities on this telephone gimmick. This would be one of them. He'd already been into the possibility I'd brought up and which he had, in talking to me, knocked down—the chance that the kidnaper might still be calling in to ask for a one- or two-day suspension of service. This was one of his possibilities. The kidnaper might call in to ask for an emergency restoration of service before the expiration of the fifteen-day period. Gibby wanted a record of any such calls as might come in and an immediate relay of that information to us.

He got that set up and then he asked his question. That one wasn't even a possibility, not if you are thinking of possibilities that could help us catch up with the kidnaper before the ransom was paid. He wanted to know whether at any time we gave them the word, they could restore service on all their temporarily disconnected telephones. Actually they couldn't. It would take time to get them all back in. I put that phase of it out of my mind. Later would be plenty of time to think of that. All that was good for was cutting down on the margin the kidnaper would be allowing himself for his getaway. We'd have to be enormously lucky for that margin to be cut sufficiently to do us any good. We might get it cut enough to make an appreciable difference in the length of Dora's and Emily's and Little Lonnie's ordeal. This last objective did seem most worth while. I was all for it but I wasn't losing sight of the fact that, desirable as it was, it was still no more than a secondary objective.

As soon as Gibby'd hung up, I was unlimbering my ax on that possibility he'd lined up.

"You don't really think he's going to make it that easy for us?" I asked. "Call in and ask for an emergency restoration of service?"

Gibby grinned at me. "Why not?" he said. "The hackie said he did it and he did care about the saving on his phone bill. This bird won't be caring about that. So they'll charge him just as though the phone had been in service all along. He couldn't care less. His plans don't call for being around to pay that bill anyhow."

"It's not the bill," I said. "It's a matter of making himself conspicuous. Calling the telephone company and saying he's got an emergency. That's making himself conspicuous. I can't picture a kidnaper doing that."

"What else can he do?" the Old Man asked me. "He *will* be having an emergency. If he failed to have the service shut off on that phone early enough, he has to handle it some way, and what other way can he have?"

If the Old Man's coffee hadn't been so bad, he might have managed to drink more of it, and I feel confident he would have been a lot sharper. Gibby was. He was in there with the answer while I was still putting words together for it.

"He can let it ride," Gibby said. "He leaves Emily and Dora and the baby locked up with the dead phone. He can have had only one reason for telling Emily about the phone trick in the first place. He was demonstrating to her that he did have a way of collecting the ransom and making a getaway that wouldn't involve doing her or anyone else any violence. He can leave it that way. She plays along. It won't be too bad. Only a day or two before she can phone out and get someone to come and let them out of there. He doesn't have to tell her he goofed and it's going to be longer than that. He just takes off and leaves her to work at that phone futilely until service finally is restored."

"Fifteen days?" the old man groaned.

"Less than that," Gibby said. "Thirteen days at most. We can assume he had the phone service cut off before he pulled the snatch. That means it will have been off at least two days come Monday. If we do that badly, we will get the phone company to put a call through on every one of their temporarily disconnected phones. Even if it does mean thousands of calls, we just leave enough of a time margin so we can be sure he'll be gone by then and it will be safe to put a call through. Then we start calling right down the list of numbers. Work with as large a team as we can get and we'll hit the right phone within a matter of hours at most."

"If Emily or Dora answer," I said.

Now the Old Man was looking at me as though he

thought I should have forced down more of that filthy coffee.

"Why in hell wouldn't they answer?" he growled.

"Suppose he's left them with orders not to touch the phone for twenty-four or forty-eight hours," I said. "We hit the phone some time Monday, let's say. Are they going to think we've pulled off a miracle for them or are they going to think it's the kidnaper checking on them and will they be afraid to answer? Think of it the way they'll think. They won't be expecting a call to come in. They'll be expecting to call out. The phone rings. We don't know where to reach them. Nobody knows that but the kidnaper. They'll play safe and not answer it. That's a good bet."

"Nonsense," the Old Man said. "We'll have told Miss Stewart that we're working on the telephones and we'll get through to her as soon as we can."

Gibby shook his head. "No," he said. "That we can't do. If it goes all the way to the end of the line that way and she has to go to this guy with the ransom money, she has to go thinking that nothing has been done by us, not anything whatsoever. She'll never be able to carry it off, if she has any idea we're doing anything toward circumventing this guy. She'll be too afraid."

The Old Man looked stricken. "But as much as thirteen days," he wailed. "We can't let her walk into anything like that. The adults might survive thirteen days of it, but there's the infant. Food supplies for a day or two. They use those up and the phone is still dead. How long can a baby go without milk?"

That pink telephone rang. The Old Man jumped.

Gibby picked it up. Before speaking into it though, he answered the Old Man.

"The phone won't be dead when they've used the food up," he said. "We're having all the temporarily disconnecteds restored to service, starting as soon as it's safe on Monday. The worst that happens is they'll wait till the time he tells them before they'll touch the phone, but when they do touch it, we'll have service for them on it. We'll have service on all the phones."

He took his hand off the mouthpiece and spoke into the phone. He wasn't on long and when he got off he was cursing.

"Now what?" the Old Man asked.

"Bronson," Gibby said. "We can pick him up now any time the cops find him. They're looking for him. They have two people who are ready to sign a complaint. The charge is simple assault. There's a man named Curtis Kendall. He alleges that Bronson beat up on him about a half hour ago. The other complainant is a woman. She says Bronson slapped her around a bit. It happened in her apartment. She's Mrs. Hulon Stewart. Not Gloria, but Susan—the first Mrs. Hulon Stewart."

Five

Sending us off with his blessing, the Old Man went back to bed. We took off without stopping to tuck him in. So far as I could see, we weren't in any great hurry. It was rather that we didn't want to wake the Old Man's wife. They do share a bedroom. I've seen it on other occasions. It's pink like the kitchen telephone. Gibby, however, was in a hurry but I laid that to his having had enough of the Old Man's company for a while. Gibby sometimes finds the Old Man rather stuffy.

I couldn't imagine that Gibby was seeing anything that could be taken for a lead in this news he'd had of Bronson's reverting to type with some man in the first Mrs. Stewart's apartment. I was even going beyond that. I remembered that Bronson had asserted with much righteous indignation that he had never struck a woman, not even a woman that wasn't his Dora. I hadn't been too much inclined to believe him then and even if I had believed him I would have felt that there always has to be a first time for anyone, even for Bud Bronson.

We had, after all, Gibby and Bronson and I, all been witnesses to Gloria Stewart's outburst of hysteria. She had made charges of a sort against her predecessor, Susan, but they hadn't been notably impressive charges and it seemed to me that, if they should have impressed anyone, Bronson shouldn't have been the one. You may remember that Gloria offered nothing to implement these charges beyond an indication that Dora Mason had come into her employ at the recommendation of the first Mrs. Stewart. It seemed to me, therefore, that one would have to believe that Dora was guiltily involved in the kidnaping before one could conceive of any sort of involvement for Mrs. Susan Stewart. I had been assuming that Bronson would be the last man to hold any such belief. Even now, as we were covering the short distance to the scene of the crime —Susan Stewart's apartment was only a few blocks away from the Old Man's, a plush neighborhood but not nearly as plush as East Sixty-second Street—I could only believe that Bronson had completely missed the connection in which Gloria had mentioned Susan and in his state of angry frustration had felt compelled to hit out at some-one. We were going over there. We were leaving no stone unturned, but I wasn't asking myself to work up any wild excitement over a routine job of stone turning. I was more interested in the telephone problem.

"I hope," Gibby was saying, "that before the Old Man goes back to bed he doesn't forget to get some men over to the phone company to start on those lists of tempo-rarily disconnected phones."

"He wasn't that sleepy," I said. "He won't forget. You said they have thousands of them. How big a job is it going to be checking them out?"

"All of them? If the Old Man puts every man he can get on it, the job will still take months."

"So we have to be just too, too lucky."

"That's about it, even though there are ways of paring it down. If the Old Man's on the ball, it shouldn't be more than an hour before they'll be ready to start on it. If we can get through with Susan by then, we'll go downtown and get them started on it ourselves. If not, I'll have to phone in and give them some ideas on short cuts."

"Like what?"

"Like doing a quick elimination on most of them."

"How?"

"All they have to do is look and most of them will drop right out as obvious impossibles."

"Look at what?"

"Where the phone is. It can't be in an apartment house. There isn't an apartment house in town that's so well soundproofed that you would have to use a telephone to let someone know that you were locked in. It would have to be a place where hammering on walls, jumping up and down on the floor, screaming, anything like that would do no good. It has to be a private house."

"Yes," I conceded. "Check directories and drop all apartment phones out of consideration. It's an apartment house town, but even so there are a lot of private houses still around."

"More than I like to think about," Gibby agreed. "But

even there we can do an elimination. It has to be a single-occupancy house. Rooming houses, houses that have been converted into two or three flats, those would also drop out."

"How would you have a temporarily disconnected phone in a rooming house? It would always have to be in service for the roomers, wouldn't it?"

"It wouldn't be a rooming-house phone," Gibby explained. "Actors, call girls, bookies, all people who use a phone a lot in making their living. People like that often take a room in a rooming house and have their own private phone installed in the room. A person like that goes away for a while. The phone is temporarily disconnected. We'll eliminate more of them that way than you think."

"What then?" I gloomed. "Even if we get it down to hundreds, where are we?"

"About to talk to the first Mrs. Stewart," Gibby said cheerfully. "We were going to have to find some way of talking to her but I couldn't figure any way that wouldn't have to wait at least till morning. We can thank Bronson for that much. He's fixed it so we don't have to wait."

"It's morning now," I muttered.

"Broad daylight morning I meant," Gibby said. "We're ahead a good five or six hours on this and the way we're crowded for time, that's a lot. On a kidnaping, Mac, any time you can pick up, even an hour, you don't knock it. Every minute counts."

Susan Stewart's place turned out to be one of those deals we'd just been discussing. She had an apartment but it was not what most people would ordinarily think of in association with the word. It wasn't a unit in a large apartment building. It was more like this deal Gibby and I have, a couple of floors in what was once a private dwelling. Hers was bigger than ours and considerably more elegant. It was many notches down the financial and social scale from the East Sixty-second Street layout occupied by her husband, her daughter, and her successor; but it was still in what I would call a more than average luxurious bracket.

The real estate name for it would be a garden apartment. In other words she had the lower floors of this house and with them went a back yard. Somebody had done up the back yard to make it more Japanese than anything I've seen this side of Sessue Hayakawa. There was a pool with water in it and to cross the pool an obviously unnecessary bridge of the up-one-side-and-down-the-other variety. The pool was so narrow that almost anyone could step across it and furthermore, if one did cross it, there was nothing to do but come back. There wasn't anything on the other side. There were rock plants and a few flowers and more than a few lanterns. All together it was a good place for putting on a performance of *Madame Butterfly* and what more appropriate for a dame whose husband has walked out on her and married another babe?

The Japanese invasion had spilled over from the garden into the apartment itself. There were paper screens around and in front of them gray jugs with a few spare branches stuck in them. A Chinese once told me that the

Japanese tea ceremony was a process of making an art out of not having enough tea and that the Japanese cult of flower arranging was similarly a process of making an art of not having enough flowers. One look at the first Mrs. Hulon Stewart and her living room, and I suddenly had a pretty sharp idea of what that Chinese had meant.

It hit you on sight. Here was a dame who had taken to making an art of not having enough of anything in her life. She was immediately recognizable as Emily Stewart's mother. It was not that when she would reach her forties Emily could be expected to look like this. They weren't the one any sort of image of the other. It was only a resemblance, but a strong one. Emily was far the prettier of the two and it was a difference that could not be laid to the difference in ages. The girl had her mother's features but, feature by feature, the girl's face and figure had been modified subtly in the direction of prettiness by something she'd had from her father.

Susan was a gaunt type. She was long-nosed and wide-mouthed and firm-chinned. There was everything about her clothes and her grooming to tell you that she had worked hard at softening the contours and at converting herself into something soft and giddy and feminine, but you could easily imagine that the very effort she'd put into it had been self-defeating. This was a hard dame with frills on.

If Bud Bronson had been slapping her around, she certainly had nothing to show for it. There were evidences of violence about but none of them were on Susan Stewart. The frame of one of her paper screens had been broken and there was a long, jagged tear across the paper. She told us that there had been other damage. One of the gray jugs had been thrown and it had shattered, but she wasn't much concerned about that. What was bothering her was the damage to Curtis Kendall.

He had been damaged. That was also immediately recognizable. Mr. Kendall looked very young. He also had that look that would tell you that, if seen in an un-damaged state, he could be very pretty. That night he had a shiner that had been developing nicely even though he was holding an ice-pack pressed against it. His nose had that puffy look noses have when their bleeding has only recently been stopped. He was dressed in a black-and-gray silk Japanese kimono which seemed almost too good a choice for his pale hair and delicately pink skin. Around his shoulders had been draped a mink cape. He was sitting on a low bench and he had his bare feet soaking in a pan of hot water. One of his hands was occupied with keeping the ice applied to his eye. The other was never still. It was occupied with twitching the recurrently slip-ping cape back up on his shoulders, raising a drink to his lips, alternating the drink with a cigarette, and filling the air with gestures of shock and indignation.

There was still a squad car outside the house when we got there and a couple of cops were inside still talking to Mrs. Stewart and Kendall. They were boys we knew and once they'd greeted us, we were automatically ac-cepted by the assembled company. I gathered quickly that we might have been similarly accepted even if there had been no cops. Mrs. Stewart seemed to be keeping open house. All of her guests were more or less masculine. I spotted two types that looked like undamaged Kendalls and classified them among the less masculine. The more masculine was represented by a character in blue jeans and a black T-shirt. Kendall and the other two might have been chorus boys. The odd one had the build and carriage of a kid who fought preliminaries in the welter-weight division but, only because he was there with the others, I figured him as more likely to be a dancer.

The chorus boys were in almost as much of a flutter as was Kendall. The muscle lounged impassively on the back of his neck and divided himself equally between yawning and working his way down through an imperial quart of straight rye. Everybody had drinks except the cops, of course, but for a party that was still going at four in the morning, nobody was noticeably drunk.

Susan tried to give us drinks and we murmured the not-on-duty formula. She said that was a bore and with a wave of her arm toward the cops she said plaintively that they weren't drinking either and told us that she was baffled at the thought of any man in these days of full employment settling for a job that would cut in on his drinking.

"Nobody's on duty all the time," I said.

"Then you'll have to come back some time when you're not," she said cordially. "That's what they're going to do. They've promised." This was accompanied by another wave of her arm toward the cops. She turned to Kendall. "Since none of them is drinking," she said, "we can't possibly run short of ice. Take all you want for your eye, darling. It will be all right."

Kendall took some more but it was for a fresh drink he was making himself.

We checked with the cops for a fill-in. What they gave us didn't sound good for much. It seemed, in fact, so strikingly poor that it was quite impossible that any police officer wouldn't have recognized that what they had was not going to go down with anybody as what might be called a satisfactory or even an adequate information. They retailed it to us in the most official, deadpan manner. I could understand that. They were just passing it on. They were taking no responsibility for it.

I can give you a quick résumé of it. It isn't worth more than that. Bud Bronson had walked in on the party and nobody had anticipated any sort of trouble. Susan Stewart, since she was the hostess, had done as she would do when any guest arrived. That it was a guest she neither recognized nor remembered asking seemed to make no difference. He had walked in and therefore he was welcome. It was as simple as that. She had gone forward, taken him by the arm, and started to lead him toward the bar. Much to her astonishment, he hadn't behaved like a guest. He had jerked his arm away, had told her that he had no time for kidding around, and had immediately turned ugly.

"The lady says he told her he didn't want any part of her or her drinks. All he wanted was information."

"He was profane and nasty about it," the lady contributed. "He was also completely incoherent. If he had been drunk, I should have known how to handle that. I understand drunks, but this was different. This man was quite sober but he was mad, obviously psychotic. I'm no psychiatrist, of course, but a child would have recognized it. A paranoiac. You know, persecution delusions and striking out blindly and all that. A textbook case."

Gibby listened politely, but at the first opportunity he turned back to the cops. As they had it, Bronson had shaken off the lady's hold on his arm and had demanded of her that she tell him where "she" was, where Susan Stewart had taken "her" or had had "her" taken.

"Her," I repeated after them. "Did he say who?"

Mrs. Stewart answered. "I had to ask him that," she said. "That's the way they are in these delusions. It's all about how they're going to fix you for what you've done to them, and when you ask them what you've done, they tell you not to play the innocent with them. You know very well what you've done."

"Did you?" Gibby asked. We had tangled with do-it-yourself psychiatrists before.

"Of course not," she answered, as though she were indulging him by belaboring for his benefit the self-evident. "One never does with these paranoid cases. One can't because one hasn't done anything. In fact nothing has been done. It's all in their minds."

The cops went on with it. Mrs. Stewart had asked him and, as she had been telling us, he'd told her that she knew well enough. He'd also told her not to play innocent with him and had driven his point home by slapping her. She had backed away from him and he had started after her. At that point he had also, after a fashion, answered a question. He had roared a girl's name at her.

"The lady don't remember the name," the cops told us, "but it looks like it was Dora."

"Dora, Bridget, one of those names. As far as I knew then, it was nobody I'd ever heard of and the man was coming after me looking really insane. I must admit I forgot the name as quickly as he said it, but Paul thinks he remembers and he says it was Dora."

"Paul?" Gibby asked.

The muscle spoke up. "That's me," he said. "Paul Galitzin. That was the name, Dora. She was going to tell him where she had Dora or he was going to choke it out of her. They should've just let him yell. He wasn't going to do anything."

"He had already struck Susan," Kendall said loftily.

"Sure. I was here. I seen it," Paul said scornfully. "So he pasted her one. If he choked her the way he socked her, it wasn't going to be anything to get in no sweat about. A guys hangs one on a broad, he don't even have to touch her nearly and he's got her marked. It's like that with broads. They got skins that mark real easy. You can see for yourself. Not a mark on her. He wasn't playing for keeps, nowhere near it."

"He hadn't started," Kendall said and he was going painfully shrill with indignation. "I wasn't waiting for him to start, not like some people."

Paul laughed lightly. "Nobody's said you ain't a hero, Kitty," he said. "Soon as the hock shops open, we'll pin a medal on you."

"Stop calling me Kitty," Kendall shrieked.

He also stamped his foot, which was a mistake. Stamping makes no effect at all when it is done barefoot. When it's done in a hot footbath, it does make an effect of sorts, but the wrong one. It's messy, not emphatic.

"Anybody else hear the name?" Gibby asked.

"I," Kendall said with an excruciating air of self-righteousness, "had no time for what he was saying. I was too much concerned with what he was doing and with saving Suekins from him."

"Suekins?"

"Mrs. Stewart."

We tried the other two. All we got out of them was their own names. Tom Jones and Joseph Andrews, so help me.

"Couldn't David Copperfield come?" I asked.

They tittered. Later, in the routine course of things, we did find out what their names had been originally. They were the sort of names one easily forgets and, since they never did matter, I've forgotten them. They were completely within their rights, though, in giving out with the literary aliases. Both had had their names legally changed.

At the time they told us, though, that they hadn't the faintest idea of what the creature had been shouting. They supposed that they had heard. It would have been impossible not to have heard because he had been roaring, but he had been so violent that they'd had no mind for just what he'd been shouting.

"It was all we could do to keep out of his way," they said.

"I suppose it was Dora," Suekins offered. "Agnes has

reminded me since that Dora was the name of the girl she got my ex for his brat. It seems this person is this Dora's boy friend. Agnes says she recognized him. If it hadn't been for Agnes, we'd never have had the first idea of who the person was, as a matter of fact. Lawrence Bronson. Agnes gave us his name."

"Who's Agnes?" I asked.

"My maid."

"And where's Agnes now?" Gibby asked.

"I expect she's gone back to bed," Suekins said with a pout. "In the morning she'll give me her notice again. Her day ends at ten o'clock and she'll do nothing for me after that. If she's so much as disturbed after ten, she's a storm cloud at breakfast and she hands me her notice. Then I have to give her something nice or raise her pay to make her stay on. It's going to be one of those mornings."

"Things," Gibby said, "are tough all over."

We returned to the cops. When we had left them, they'd had Bronson pursuing Mrs. Stewart across her living room and demanding that she tell him what she had done with Dora. Mrs. Stewart had retreated all the way back to her Japanese garden when Kendall intervened. He shot a foot out, as Bronson came charging by, and tripped Bronson neatly.

He'd had very little assistance. Paul, the muscle, who from the first had taken no more interest than might be mustered for such a situation by an aloof connoisseur of violence, had throughout maintained his role of amused spectator. It had been his judgment that Bud Bronson was not playing for keeps. Even though the blows Bronson landed on Kendall were not so gentle that they didn't mark our hero, it was evident that Paul had considered them to be more or less negligible. Paul suggested, in fact, that anytime he wanted to he could do better himself with that proverbial one hand tied behind his back.

Jones and Andrews, in their way, had been more helpful. They had run out to the street and yelled for the cops, and Suekins had been of similar assistance. She had also yelled for the cops, but by telephone. Meanwhile Bronson had been pummeling Kendall and had finally disposed of him by picking him up bodily and tossing him into that little ornamental pool out in the Japanese back garden.

Returning from the garden, he had been apparently ready to resume his inquiries; but, even if in his bemused state he might have disregarded Mrs. Stewart's activities at the telephone, even he wasn't so much bemused that he could ignore the caterwauling Tom and Joseph had set up out in front of the house. Cursing the company individually and collectively as he went, Bronson had taken off. The police had been there quickly but not quickly enough. Bronson hadn't waited for them.

"Then he never did really get around to telling you what he wanted?" Gibby asked.

"He wanted Dora."

"Did he give you any idea of what made him think you might have her here?"

"Now, really. One doesn't expect anything as reasonable as that from a disturbed paranoid."

"Did he say anything about a kidnaping?"

"A kidnaping?" Mrs. Stewart laughed. "That big horse of a girl? He was insane but not that insane."

"Lonnie?"

Susan Stewart registered astonishment. If Gibby had been after a reaction, he had it. If anything, it was almost too much. Her whole body stiffened. Her eyes blinked. Her jaw dropped. She held it for a long moment and then a glint of malicious laughter showed in her eyes and her lips twitched.

"My ex?" she said eagerly. "Not my ex and the nurse-maid? Don't tell me they've gone off together?" She crossed her arms over her bosom and grabbed at her shoulders. She was hugging herself and it could have been because quite abruptly she had begun shaking. It also could have been a paroxysm of wild glee. Which-ever it was, she did behave as though it were the latter. "Now get this, everybody," she gasped. "My precious ex is tired of Gloria already. Now he's climbing back up the social ladder. Dora, the nursemaid, his first step on the road back."

Jones and Andrews hooted gently. Paul poured himself another slug of rye and tossed it off. He looked like a man who had tasted something he didn't like and was washing the taste out of his mouth. Kendall showed no sign of having heard any of it. He was dipping a finger in his footbath and complaining that the water had gone cold and that the least he was going to get would be pneumonia.

It was at that point that Agnes joined the party. A

door I hadn't noticed before swung open a few inches and she popped her head around the edge of it. It was a forbidding sort of head, elderly, thin-lipped, and scornful-looking. The hair was iron-gray and it was rolled up tight on metal curlers. The effect was chilling and steely, as though she had buckled on a helmet in readiness to do battle.

"You want more water," she growled, "ask for it."

"This is cold," Kendall complained.

"You already said that. You want more hot water?"

"Please."

The head withdrew and the door swung shut.

"Agnes?" Gibby asked.

Mrs. Stewart nodded. She had no mind for the maid.

"Tell me everything," she said. "Every last thing dear Lonnie has been up to."

"How has he been doing with his alimony payments?" Gibby asked.

"He's been paying them. What else would he do? The boy can be difficult but not about money. That's one fault he's never had. There's not much good I can say about him, but there is that. Lonnie's generous. Why do you ask? Is Gloria worried? She needn't be. He'll be generous to her, too. That's Lonnie."

The door swung open again. This time it came all the way and all of Agnes came around it. The rest of her was wrapped in a gray toweling bathrobe and she was shuffling along in a pair of gray toweling mules. She moved with too much vigor for it, but otherwise she looked like an ambulatory patient in the ward of a charity hospital. She was carrying a steaming kettle and she headed straight for Kendall and his footbath.

"You're talking too much again," she muttered at Mrs. Stewart, as she went past. "I've told you a hundred times. You'll do better not talking so much." Tipping her kettle, she let the boiling water pour into the footbath. Kendall screamed. She tipped the kettle up and held it poised as though she were menacing him with it. "What's the matter with you?" she said.

"You're scalding me."

"It won't do you any good unless it's good and hot," she said. "You should have mustard in it anyway. It's a waste of time without mustard."

"I don't want mustard."

"You don't know what you want but I don't care."

"We're from the District Attorney's office, Agnes," Gibby said, introducing himself and me.

Agnes set the kettle down on the floor beside Kendall. "Put it in for yourself when you want it," she said, "but what you ought to do is go home and go to bed."

"Are my clothes dry yet?"

"Your clothes won't be dry until tomorrow. One of them can go and get you some dry stuff, can't they?"

She indicated Jones and Andrews. They giggled.

"He will sleep here tonight, Agnes," Mrs. Stewart said with an attempt at firmness.

"Sleep?" Agnes sneered. "Nobody sleeps." She turned to us. "So you're from the District Attorney's office," she said. "What's that supposed to make me do? Drop dead?"

"Mrs. Stewart tells us you recognized the man," I said.

"Him? Lawrence Bronson. And anybody who isn't more than half a fool would have known all along it had to happen. First time I saw him I knew, so it's nothing to go making a federal case about."

"You knew what?" Gibby asked.

"What everybody knows. You don't go taking up with a drinking man unless you like them that way. I told Dora right off, but she thinks she's smarter than anybody. Nobody else can do it but that isn't because it can't be done. It's because everybody else isn't Dora Mason. If Dora Mason puts her mind to it, she can do anything. Now she knows. She put him on the wagon. She's kept him there. It's been months now. So what? I don't care. It can be years but it's got to come. One day he falls off, but good. Today was the day."

"You think he'd been drinking?"

"What else?"

"We saw him less than an hour before he got here," Gibby said. "He hadn't been drinking then. He didn't have the time in between to get drunk enough to matter."

"He wasn't drunk at all," Susan Stewart volunteered. "If there is one thing I know, it's drunks."

"You sure do," Agnes said grimly, "or you ought to."

"What do you know about Bronson except that he used to drink?" Gibby asked.

"If I know anything about him you don't know, mister," Agnes said, "then I've got something to ask you. What do we pay taxes for? That's what I want to know. That Lawrence Bronson has been in and out of jail I don't know how many times. There isn't a cop anywhere in town who doesn't know him and you come from the District Attorney's office to ask me what I know about him. Don't you know anything?"

Gibby grinned at her. "Not nearly as much as you do, Agnes," he said. "For instance, tell me this. You know about his record. Does Dora know?"

"Of course she knows. The first time she ever set eyes on him and she went dancing with him, everybody told her. But that's Dora. It's like with his drinking. All he needs, she says, is somebody to keep him toeing the mark and she's the somebody to do it. She's got him working regular. She's got him off the bottle. She's reforming him all around, making a new man of him. Now she'll get some sense."

"Where did she meet him?"

"At this dance. It was a club dance and he come over and asked her. She let him take her home."

"You know how these girls are," Mrs. Stewart offered. "There are always these dances they go to where they pick up men."

"Sure," Agnes said. "You can do it at a dance or you can do it in the bank or in a taxicab or in a saloon where they keep it dark enough so they can call it a cocktail lounge."

Mrs. Stewart caught her lip between her teeth. "Agnes," she said. "You're going too far."

"I know," Agnes said calmly. "You're thinking about firing me again. I'm not worried. Any time you're ready. It's all right with me. You need me a lot more than I need you and don't try telling me I don't know what's what." She glowered at Kendall. "That one," she said.

"He clerks in the bank. First it's he comes here after work for cocktails. Then it's they're going to dinner and they're going to the theater and they're going dancing afterward and in his bank there isn't even a shortage in the cash. So how can that be? It can be because he never pays for anything. Everywhere she signs the checks. Dora, when she picked up a man, she had sense enough to pick one who pays the carfare."

"I'm warning you, Agnes," Mrs. Stewart said feebly.

"I'm warning *you,"* Agnes came back at her and there was nothing feeble in her attack. "Don't you go talking about how these girls are. You picked that one up in the bank." She turned from Kendall to glower at Jones and Andrews. "Them," she growled. "They came to hang the curtains and they stayed to dinner. Now every time they get thirsty, they fall in here. And him—" She pointed a stubby, work-roughened finger at Paul Galitzin, as her voice rose to a summit of outrage. "Let me tell you how she found that one. One day she rode in his cab. She asked him when he was knocking off. Two in the morning he goes in. So she tells him to drop around for a drink. That was the first time. That was two months ago and he's been one of our regulars ever since. It'll take him another half hour to get to the bottom of that bottle and then he'll go home to his wife and kids. It's a saloon we've got here. Two o'clock every morning they come home from dancing, her and the boy friend. After that the door is open and everybody falls in. It's a saloon."

"I warned you," Susan Stewart screamed at her. "This time you've done it. You're through."

"I'm not through. There's her ex. He doesn't go to dances looking for girls. He goes to night clubs. It costs more but it's better because the girls are naked and when they dance past him he reaches out and pinches one on the leg. So she gets to be the second Mrs. Hulon Stewart and she eats her breakfast in bed."

Susan Stewart rushed at her and swung, but it was evident that they'd done that before. Agnes was ready for it. She fended off the slap and caught Mrs. Stewart by the wrists. There was a brief struggle but Agnes had a firm grip and, after a couple of moments, Mrs. Stewart crumpled and began crying. She cried like a child, sobbing wildly. Agnes gathered her into her arms and comforted her. She told her that she was just tired and that everything would be all right.

"Come now," she said. "Come now, dear. I'll put you to bed and you'll sleep and everything will look better tomorrow. Come, dear. Come with Agnes."

Susan Stewart went. We were left with her strange assortment of cavaliers. They didn't even look startled.

"This the way the parties usually finish?" Gibby asked.

"Two or three times a month," Joseph Andrews said, answering the question. "Most nights we don't even see Agnes. She's gone to bed and she doesn't get up. It's only once in a while when Sue goes to pieces and Agnes has to get up and put her to bed. They always have this first. It's like family fights. It follows a pattern."

"Agnes has worked for her a long time?"

Andrews nodded. "Agnes worked for her mother," he said. "When Sue married, Agnes went with her. Sue has a daughter, Emily. When Sue and Stewart split up, Emily chose to stay with her father. Agnes had been the girl's baby nurse and I guess, when the girl outgrew her, Agnes went back to babying Sue. It's been going on ever since. She's half mother and half maid."

"He's had a baby with the new one," Tom Jones offered. "He tried to get Agnes to walk out on this and go back over there to take care of the new baby. Not a prayer. She's always talking about how she's going to quit but she'll never quit. They'll both cry a while now, and then Sue will fall asleep and Agnes will come back down here to put us out. That is if we're still here. Sometimes we disappoint her by not waiting for it."

"Any of you know the other girl?" Gibby asked.

"The daughter? Emily?" Jones said.

It wasn't what Gibby had been asking, but he let it stand.

"We've seen her," Andrews said.

"It's over the girl that Sue is always having these fights with the old bag," Paul contributed. "This is the first time it ain't been over Emily."

"What do they fight about usually?"

"Emily, like I've been telling you. Emily's got this boy friend she can't bring home. She brings him here. Her mother thinks it's the nuts. The old bag says it's for the birds. They tangle about it every time."

"Why can't she bring him home?"

It was my question. I expect Gibby would have asked it but I didn't wait. It seemed to me too peculiar a picture of that household on East Sixty-second. I couldn't picture Hulon Stewart as the stern, old-fashioned father.

Kendall stood up in his pan of water. "It isn't anybody's business," he said. "Why can't you all shut up?"

"Maybe you'll try shutting me up, Kitty?" Paul growled. "You done so good already tonight. Maybe you want to take me on."

"I just don't think it's right," Kendall said primly.

"Nuts," said Paul. He turned back to us. "You seen Gloria? She's the second Mrs. — a dish. She never looks natural with clothes on. She ain't even as old as Emily and until Stewart came along and she made her fortune by letting him pinch her tail, she was running around with this younger guy. She ditches him for Stewart, so when he turns up dating her new stepdaughter, she don't like it. A dame that's made good like Gloria done, she don't want nobody from the past coming around to remind her. That's the half of it. The other half is Stewart. You get a rich creep like him. He dumps his wife to marry a babe she's younger even than his own daughter. Is he ever going to feel sure that the new wife's ex-boy friend is ex enough? He doesn't want any of that coming back to haunt him."

"Complicated," Gibby murmured. "And Emily brings Gloria's ex-boy friend here?"

"Wilfred, for jumping sakes," Paul said. "Wilfred Clark. Agnes, compared to him, she likes us. Agnes thinks he's a pimp and the old bag may not be too far wrong on that."

"There's nothing wrong with the man," Kendall said loftily. "You can't blame Sue for finding it all too amusing. Gloria, wanting to have her cake and eat it, too, and just furious that Wilfred can be anything less than completely heartbroken over her. And Stewart, the old fool, simply livid with fear that if Emily keeps bringing Wilfred around, the old flame will rekindle in Gloria and all that. Of course Sue encourages Emily. It keeps Gloria and Stewart in a ferment and that makes Sue feel that she's getting a little of her own back. What's so wrong with that?"

"Your big mouth's wrong with it," Agnes snarled as she came back into the room carrying a heap of rumpled clothes. She dropped them on the floor beside Kendall. "Put those on and get out of here. I'm going to lock up."

"They're still damp," Kendall protested.

"So wear them damp or go home in the kimono. See if I care."

"Sue said I was to stay the night."

"She's asleep and I'm telling you to go home."

It was obvious that this also had happened before or something enough like it so that Kendall recognized that he had no appeal from Agnes' decision. Grumbling, he picked up his clothes and went out of the room with them. He did allow himself one small touch of defiance. He went without stopping to dry his feet and when Agnes screamed about the puddles he was leaving on the floor, he let her scream. In scooping up his clothes, however, he had left his shirt. Agnes spotted it and she stopped screaming. Using it, she sopped up the water from the floor. Then going to the door through which he had vanished, she pulled it open and threw the shirt in after him.

The others pulled themselves together and took off. They weren't waiting for her to get around to putting them out. We let them go. Agnes locked the doors that opened on the little Japanese garden. She headed for the front door. On her way by she spoke to us.

"Out," she said. "I'm locking up."

"You'll have to wait till Kendall's dressed," Gibby told her. "You can tell us a few things while you're waiting."

"Like what? Like why that Clark fellow's no fit company for a young girl? She's Emily Stewart and she ought to be a lady and you can't be a lady if you go picking up with the leavings of your father's whore. I've told her mother that and I've told her that. Anything else you want to know?"

"You found Dora Mason for Mr. Stewart. How well do you know her?"

"Like she was my own daughter."

"Then she can be trusted?"

"I don't put an innocent baby in the hands of anyone who can't be trusted. Even if it's the whore's baby, it's not the poor little thing's fault."

"You used to be a baby nurse yourself?"

"Emily. I brought them home from the hospital. I brought her up."

"And she stayed with her father. She didn't come with you and her mother."

"She stayed where the money was. I couldn't keep him from giving her money even when she was too little. I did my best, but he spoiled her. She can't live without money."

"No money here?"

"Alimony and it's plenty and there would have been an allowance for Emily and that would have been more than plenty, but not like what she has staying with him. There it's the allowance and extras and the bribes."

"Bribes?"

"Sure. Stop seeing Wilfred Clark and I'll get you a new car. I didn't get you that new car for Wilfred Clark to drive it. Stop seeing him and you can have a new fur coat. That's the way it goes."

"Stewart, he's a pretty weak sort of character?"

"Soft. Rotten soft."

"Tell me. Do you know if he has any enemies, anyone who would want to do him a really bad turn?"

"That he has," Agnes said. "Me. Him and his free hand. He comes over everybody else. No matter what it is, he'll write a check for it. I've had his checks. He doesn't come over me. A man's got to have something more in him than money."

"His baby has been kidnaped," Gibby told her. "The child's gone and Dora with him."

Agnes looked skeptical. "You said Bronson wasn't drunk," she muttered.

"He wasn't. Dora's been kidnaped and he's looking for her."

Agnes wasn't convinced. "Why him? Why not the cops and the FBI? Why not you?"

"Because there's been a ransom demand and they've been told to keep away from the police if they want the child back alive."

"And he comes here thinking we've done it?"

"He's afraid of what might be happening to Dora. He's so afraid he's more than half crazy with it. He'll be going everywhere and anywhere."

"And you come here, too. What are you half crazy with?"

"Lack of information," Gibby said. "Worry about Bronson. He can make enough noise for this to get to the papers. If anything is printed about it now, that baby just could be killed."

Agnes softened. "Look," she said, "even if it is her baby, it's like I said. He's still a baby and not his fault. I'll tell you anything, anything you think will help; but you keep asking about Emily and like that."

"The kidnaper has been in touch with Emily. He's picked her to deliver the ransom money to him and recover Dora and the baby. She wants to do it with no police to help her or watch her or anything. She's not afraid."

Agnes raised her head. "I told you," she said. "I brought the girl up. He spoiled her with his money but some of what I did stuck. She wouldn't be afraid."

"Bronson came here looking for Dora. Where else would he go to look?"

"I don't know where he'd go. I don't know why he came here. It's up to you to stop him. You say the kidnaper talked to Emily. He picked her for the one he'll deal with. That means it's someone who knows about them. It can be all right."

"How does that figure?"

"Anyone who knows about them, has to know that Stewart will pay. Whatever they're asking, he'll pay it. Knowing that, they'll keep Dora and the baby safe, won't they? They will unless you can't catch up with Bronson and keep him quiet. Nothing else can spoil it, only that."

Six

WE PULLED OUT OF THERE and we checked with the police. The word had gone out and every patrolman in town had an eye out for Bud Bronson. The detectives were also out. They were running a check on all of Bronson's known hangouts and they were talking to people all over town, but Bronson had dropped out of sight. They didn't have even a lead on him. I found it disappointing, but it didn't knock me out. There hadn't been all that much time since Bronson had gone slamming out of Susan Stewart's place. The boys would turn him up eventually. Meanwhile there was a bit of encouragement. Up to that point things had been holding still. There hadn't been any reporters around asking embarrassing questions. There had been no intermission in the poker game in the pressroom at Police Headquarters. Whatever Bud Bronson had been doing with his time after throwing his weight around with Susan Stewart and Curtis Kendall, he had been doing it quietly and possibly even discreetly. That was so much to the good.

I said as much to Gibby. He didn't look happy about it.

"I don't like his dropping out of sight this way, Mac," Gibby said. "I don't like the smell of it."

"It's a big town and it's his town," I said. "There's a million places he could have gone to hole up. The boys'll get some info on him and in time they'll dig him out. You know this game. Do I have to tell you we can't expect them to bring it off in an hour?"

"Not if he's holed up, but that's the one thing he wasn't doing tonight."

"Not until he overreached himself at Mrs. Stewart's. He pulled out of there one jump ahead of the cops. What was there for him to do then except hole up?"

"And forget Dora?"

"And figure he couldn't do anything for Dora once he'd been tucked away in the pokey."

"Reasonable," Gibby muttered, "except that he wasn't in a reasonable mood. He was in a world-well-lost-for-love mood. He was in a mood for taking the big chances, resorting to the desperate measures. I'd be happier if we knew where he's gone to take them."

It was a disquieting thought and one about which we could do nothing. I worked at talking Gibby out of it, but mainly because I was trying to talk myself out of it. We went down to the phone company where the check-out of the temporarily disconnected telephones had begun. Just on theory that had seemed a pretty unpromising approach. Confronted with the huge stacks of material that would have to be sifted for the city alone, I found it almost impossible to see any hope for it and that without even allowing myself to think of the possibility, or even likelihood, that it would be an out-of-town number.

We did make a couple of suggestions on procedure, but I doubt that Gibby had much more faith in them than I had, which was close to none at all. We didn't hang around there long. The job was being done, so far as it could be done, and it wasn't any good hanging around and watching it. Before we pulled out we called in to headquarters again and checked on how the hunt for Bud Bronson was going. It was going strong but it was still without results.

That seemed to wash us up for the night but, when we came out into the street, we saw that the night itself was washed up. Daylight had begun seeping into the city. We headed uptown. There wasn't going to be much sleep for us but, even if it would be only an hour or two, it did seem smart to catch us what we could. On our way downtown we had picked up Gibby's car and he had driven a couple of blocks past our street before I even noticed. When I did notice, I sat up and called him on it.

"I know," he said. "I thought we'd just go around through Sixty-second and then we'll go home and hit the sack."

"What for Sixty-second?"

Gibby shrugged. "Just for a look at the house," he said. "See if they're still all lit up."

"What if they are?"

He laughed. "Now that you ask me," he said, "I don't know what."

"Then make a U-turn and let's go home."

"We've come this far. It'll be only a minute more."

"To no purpose," I growled.

"To no purpose," he agreed, "except that I have the itch to do it. If we don't, I'll be too itchy to get to sleep."

I yawned. "They sell insecticides for that," I said.

We bowled into East Sixty-second. The whole street was dark and that included the Stewart house. The curbs were lined with parked cars just the way they always are in almost any Manhattan street. Earlier in the evening the parking had been not quite solid. Now you could see that all the householders in the neighborhood had returned from their Saturday night entertainments. Both curbs were filled solidly and in front of the Stewart house there was a snappy-looking station wagon double parked.

We spotted that from the end of the street. Gibby pulled to a stop. That put us double parked maybe fifty yards away.

"The station wagon," Gibby said.

"What about it?"

"It wasn't there before."

"Neither were a lot of these other cars."

"I know, but the others aren't double parked."

"We are."

"We got here late."

"So did the station wagon."

"Somebody making a late call at the Stewarts'."

"Or in the house across the street or in any other house along the block."

"No," Gibby said. "When you're double parking, one place is as good as another or as bad. You double park when you're not going to be long and you automatically pick a spot right in front of where you're going. Somebody's gone into the Stewart house for just a minute or two."

"So what? It's not a contact. You don't have kidnapers dropping around in person to set up preliminary arrangements for ransom payment. If it's anybody, it's a doctor. They had to break down and get one for Gloria."

"Two things wrong with that," Gibby said. "It isn't an MD license on the station wagon and there isn't a light showing anywhere in the house. A doctor wouldn't be taking care of her in the dark."

"In one of the back rooms," I suggested.

"I don't think so."

"So what do we do now? Park here till it's time to go around to the Union League?"

"Wait the few minutes it will take to see who comes out of the house."

We waited and no one came out of the house. From where we were sitting we couldn't see the sidewalk. The parked cars had that screened away from us, but we could see the front steps of all the houses right down the length of the street. If anyone came down any of those steps we couldn't fail to see him. No one came out of the Stewart house and no one came out of any of the other houses along the row. When the lights of the station wagon came on, I was completely unprepared for that. I hadn't thought of this possibility and even after I'd seen it, I couldn't make it seem a possibility.

The only thing I could figure was that someone had been sitting in that parked station wagon all along and had finally decided to move on. How do you make sense of that? It would have to be a man who had been waiting for someone, but no one had come out of any of the houses to join him in the station wagon. Someone could have come down the street, walking along behind the parked cars. Coming that way and getting into the station wagon, he would have made it without our seeing him, but then you had to ask why. As Gibby had said, you can't explain double parking and then walking all the way off the block to go some place around the corner.

The lights came on and the station wagon took off in a racing start. Gibby took off after it. It roared down to the corner and there it made a screaming turn uptown into the avenue. We screamed around the corner after it.

"What the hell goes?" I shouted.

"We're going to find out," Gibby said grimly, ramming his foot down harder on the gas.

"Nobody came out of any of the houses," I said.

"Which could mean that whoever it is in the station wagon saw us and gave up waiting," Gibby muttered.

I had what struck me as a better idea. "It could also mean," I said, "that somebody's been having a big Saturday night. He's driving home and he can't make it. He pulls up and he sleeps a while, getting himself back to the place where he can drive again."

"Drive like that?" Gibby scoffed. "This guy's crazy enough to be a drunken driver but not one just awakened from a drunken sleep. That would be unsteady. It would probably be cautious. This is steady and it's reckless."

"Somebody could have come along the street and gotten into the station wagon," I said. "We wouldn't have seen him with that solid line of parked cars in the way. We were figuring all along on seeing him as he came down the steps but not on the sidewalk or when he would be coming between the cars at the curb to get to the station wagon."

"Possible, but why does he drive this way?"

"A drunk or a nut," I said, warming to my theory. "You have a drunk. He double parks. He gets out and only then he discovers he's parked in the wrong place. He doesn't think to get back in the car and drive around to where he wants to be. He walks around, leaving the car where he's parked it. Later he comes back and takes off and we didn't see him because he didn't come from any house along the street. He came from some place around the corner."

Up to this time we'd been screaming straight up the avenue. The station wagon had been shooting along in complete disregard of speed limits or traffic lights, and Gibby had been keeping us on its tail all the way. You have to keep it in mind that this was about dawn of a Sunday morning. Any other time of day or week there would have been some little traffic to make it impossible, but even at that hour and on a Sunday it was the kind of luck that couldn't hold for long. There was going to come that intersection where some car would be crossing the avenue on a green light.

After about twenty blocks of this crazy ride we went

whamming past a police car. It did a quick U-turn and came roaring up behind us with its siren going.

"That had better be some cops who know my license," Gibby said.

"We can pull up," I suggested, "and let them take it from here."

The police car pulled abreast of us and I was looking for them to start edging us toward the curb, but they didn't. We got a wave as they went by. They knew Gibby's license. The station wagon took a quick right at the next corner, sliding out from under the nose of the police car. The cops went on through the intersection and, while they were pulling up to come around and take up the chase again, Gibby stayed with it. We'd been far enough back for him to see the turn in time.

The station wagon careened into a one-way street, the wrong way. As we came blasting through after them, it was only noticing that the parked cars flicking past on either side of us were all headed the wrong way that told me that we were careening hell-bent for the East River on a westbound street. The police-car siren swelled behind us and then I heard another come up ahead. Another squad car had picked it up and was closing in to head off the station wagon.

What I could hear could also be heard up ahead in that station wagon. It veered and sideswiped a whole row of parked cars as it ground to a stop. Gibby pulled out to clear them and he got us stopped without hitting anything. The second prowl car came turning in from the avenue ahead of us. The trap was closing. The doors of the station wagon flung open and a man came jumping out on each side.

They hit the pavement and started running. A warning shot came from the police car up ahead. As we piled out, I saw them stop dead at the shot and come doubling back toward us. It did occur to me that there was the other police job behind us and, if the boys back there had any ideas about getting off any shots, we were right in the line of fire.

It was just as well that I had no time for thinking about it. It was a nasty thought. The two were coming straight at us and they were going to meet us just where the street bottlenecked. Between Gibby's car and the bulk of that station wagon, the way they had left it, there wasn't any room for dodging. The chips were down.

Gibby and I stood shoulder to shoulder. The two came at us with their heads down. I suppose they had it figured that they could bear us down and charge right over us or that, whether they could or not, it was all they had left to try. They didn't have even that left. I don't claim to be the old hand at this sort of thing that Gibby is. Back in the days when he was working his way through law school on the cops, the nearest thing to this that I knew was football; but that's an education of sorts, too, and since then, working in team with Gibby, I've been having some postgraduate studies. It was a spot that called for a little of our higher education. Just before they hit us, we moved, pulling apart just enough to give them a spot of daylight between us.

It's automatic. They both headed in to blast through

that hole we'd given them. It was hardly enough hole for one, much less for two. They met with crashing contact that didn't fall much short of taking them out of play. We were there to handle the rest of it. I got a foot in and tripped mine up. Gibby came in with his shoulder and dropped his on top of mine. They hadn't even begun unscrambling that before the police were coming in from both ends. They saw the cops and they didn't even try to get up. They stayed down where they were and blubbered.

"We didn't," one of them wailed, "we didn't have no part of it."

"We stole the car," the other one yammered. "That's all. We only stole it."

A couple of the officers got them by the scruffs of their necks and yanked them to their feet. I'd seen it before, far too much of it, and I can say I'm past breaking my heart over it. I don't expect I'll ever get so much hardened that I'll be past the place where it kicks me in the gut, even if only a little.

Kids, burr-cut, rosy-cheeked kids. They're fifteen or sixteen even if they are big and husky. It shows in their faces. They haven't even begun being men yet.

The cops who were holding them shook them up a little.

"You only stole it?" one of the cops growled. "Ain't that enough for you? What more do you want?"

"We didn't know," the kids wailed.

"You didn't know you're not supposed to steal cars? You didn't know there's a law about that?"

"We didn't know they was in it."

That meant nothing to the cops. It meant more than I like thinking about to us. Gibby made a dive for the station wagon. I was right there with him. They were in the back on the floor and they were covered with a dark blanket. There was only the one hand that stuck out and it was a woman's hand. There was a ring on the fourth finger and it had a smallish diamond in it. The fire of the diamond jumped at us when one of the officers turned a prowl-car searchlight to beam into the back of the station wagon. The light picked up more than the ring. It picked up broken nails and on the forefinger and third finger an encrustation that looked like blood under the nails.

Gibby reached in and pulled back the blanket. There were the two of them, a man and a woman, and they were both dead. They hadn't been dead too long. The bodies were cold but no more than that, and there wasn't going to be any problem about identification. The man we knew. It was Bud Bronson. Lawrence Bronson, if you like. I suppose I should call him by his right name, giving him that much dignity in death. Dora Mason would have wanted it and in a detail like that there is every reason for respecting Dora Mason's wishes. There wasn't much more than that we could do for Dora Mason because she was also dead. It was Dora's body under that blanket with Bronson's. The diamond was the one he'd told us about, the diamond he had bought for her on time, the one that wasn't even hot. It wasn't a good enough identification for the official records, of course, but for our own information it was plenty. Bronson had shown us a picture of his Dora. This was the girl.

"Bring that pair of punks over here," Gibby said grimly.

The officers hustled the two kids over to the station wagon. They had to drag them. The kids didn't want to look.

"We didn't know they were in it," they kept protesting.

"Murder," Gibby said implacably, "murder and kidnaping. What have you done with the kid?"

"We don't know about no kid. We don't know about them even. We only stole it. If we'd have known they was in it, we wouldn't have touched it. Honest we wouldn't."

"Where did you steal it?"

"In Sixty-second Street. You seen us. The minute we started up, you seen us. You come right after us."

"What were you doing in Sixty-second Street?"

"Nothing."

"Murder and kidnaping," Gibby repeated.

The kids looked at each other. "We don't know nothing about no murder and kidnaping."

"Start knowing," Gibby said softly, "or God help you."

"You seen us steal it. You took out after us."

"What were you doing in Sixty-second Street?"

They looked at each other again. One of them started retching. The officer that had him pulled him aside and held him while he vomited. The other one stood fast for a moment or two and then he broke.

"We was looking for a car we could swipe," he said.

He'd hung his head and he was mumbling the words. He was only barely understandable.

"And out of a street full of parked cars, you just happened to pick that one?"

"When you're stealing cars, them are the ones you pick."

"I learn something every day," Gibby growled. "Never steal a car unless it's got stiffs in it. What are you trying to give us?"

"Not the stiffs. We didn't know there was stiffs. We wouldn't have touched it if we knew about the stiffs. We ain't crazy."

Kids who go prowling the streets at daybreak, looking for a car to steal—I don't know whether they're crazy or not. We can call it a matter of degree. This boy worked at convincing us. He wanted us to believe that they weren't kidnapers and they weren't killers. They were simply a pair of knowing and accomplished automobile thieves. Once he got going, he gave out with what amounted to a lecture in the techniques of car stealing.

For a boy who is at all clever about locks, it is possible to steal a car even if it is locked. Obviously, however, an unlocked car is far easier. Even easier than that is the unlocked car which has been left parked with the key not removed from the ignition. Almost any boy knows enough about wiring to jump the ignition and start a car that way if he has to, but then again that is more difficult than having the ignition key.

A boy who is really smart about stealing cars walks along looking for one that has been left unlocked and with the key in the ignition. In such a quest a car that is standing double-parked is often a good bet. A man pulls up and leaves his car that way and it often means that he's planning to be gone only a moment. It can be that he's been in enough of a hurry to forget about locking car doors and about taking the key with him.

Find one like that and it's a cinch. You don't even have to get it away from the curb. It's already standing out in the open with a clear street ahead of it. You can jump in and you're off. No monkeying around, minimal hazard.

They had come up the street, looking for an unlocked car. They kept protesting that we must have seen them as they went along trying the car doors. We didn't give them anything like telling them we wouldn't have seen them because they would have been screened from us by the cars parked along the curb. There was no telling whether they were aware of that and were using it to build their story, but it did seem as though they didn't know it because they did keep insisting that we must have seen them approach the station wagon.

It did seem likely that they had no clear idea of where we had sprung from and evidently it hadn't occurred to them that, since we had been screened from them by the line of parked cars, they had—if they were telling the truth—by the same token been screened from us.

All the cars along the curb had been locked and when they'd come to the station wagon, they slipped out between two of the parked cars and they tried the door on that. It wasn't locked. They looked in and saw the key in the ignition. That was perfect. They piled in and took off. It wasn't till they were around the corner and headed up the avenue that they even knew we were behind them and even then they didn't know we were giving chase. It was only when they kept upping their speed and we still hung on their tail that they began worrying and then the one who wasn't driving had kneeled on the seat so that he could watch and see if we were coming up on them any.

The kid who'd been vomiting gave us this part of it. He was the one who hadn't been driving and, kneeling on the seat, he'd looked down for a moment and he'd seen the hand with the ring on it. He'd leaned over and pulled back the blanket a bit. It hadn't taken much. His hand had touched one of the bodies and he had known.

"I told Ed," he sobbed. "I told him there was stiffs back there. I told him we had to lose you. We had to lose you for long enough so we could stop and we could wipe things off so they wouldn't be our fingerprints on nothing. It wasn't going to be no good unless we had time to do that before we left the car and the stiffs and got ourselves lost. Then the siren started up and it was cops after us, too."

By this time, of course, we had a street full of stuff. We let the police officers have the kids. Ed, of course, had started it, but Sam, the other one, was right in there with him. They were working so hard at giving themselves good characters as a pair of innocent car thieves that they were volunteering full lists of all previous jobs they'd pulled off. We weren't that much interested in automobile thefts. We moved on to the station wagon. It was a bit battered now, but it was still a beauty. It was one of those special body jobs and it had on it all those extras nobody ever needs. That was a station wagon that was every bit as elegant as any hearse. I asked one of the cops whether a check had been started on the station wagon registration. It was a superfluous question. The check was already in progress and I remembered how many times Gibby has accused me of underestimating the police.

"They never miss out on routine," he keeps telling me. "You can always leave that to them."

I did have the thought that I might repeat that advice back at him because it seemed to me that examination of the bodies and of the station wagon would also be a matter of routine. That also was for the police except the part that would be for the Medical Examiner; and that latter part would, in any event, hardly be anything Gibby could handle himself.

I had the thought but I held back on it. I've been out on these things with Gibby too often and he had that look. When he has that look, there isn't anyone who'll ever convince him that he isn't on to something that needs his own immediate, personal attention.

"Shot?" I asked.

"Looks like it," he answered. "On Dora it's a sure thing because it was at close range. You can see the powder marks. I haven't found any powder marks on Bronson and I don't want to maul him around looking for wounds, but it's a good enough guess that he was shot, too."

"If you're looking for powder marks on him," I said, "you aren't going to find them down there."

"Down there" was Bronson's shoes and the cuffs of his pants. Gibby was doing a really serious job of examining the shoes and turning out the pants cuffs.

"I'm finding something else," he said.

"What?"

"Sand. Beach sand and not any that was lugged to some construction job somewhere. This is sand he picked up on a beach."

I looked at the sand. It was there and there was quite a bit of it. It was stuck to the bottoms of his shoes and it was stuck in the space where the soles are fastened to the uppers. The pants cuffs were just about filled with it. There was enough of it so there could be a sample for the police lab and the boys down there might come up with some answers on it like this sample was picked up straight from a beach. Recognizing it as that on sight was something else again.

"Now," I said, "you sound like a kid on his first investigation and he's boned up for it by reading Sherlock Holmes. It's sand. It could be off a beach. It could be from a construction job. It could be out of some child's sandbox."

"When you find a couple of bits of seaweed in it, Dr. Watson, it's from a beach."

"And when we last saw him he wasn't trailing any sand around," I muttered contritely. "I took special notice of the kind of shine he had on his shoes for going around to see Dora. It was perfect. So we know that much. Between then and now he's been on a beach."

"And that's the best break we've had yet," Gibby said. "We need a phone."

"There's an all-night hamburger bar around the corner," one of the officers volunteered. "There's a booth in there."

Gibby took off on the run. I stayed with the station wagon and looked at the sand, wondering who it might be who couldn't wait to be told that Bud Bronson some time during his last hours on earth had been to the beach.

Maybe I would have found the answer for myself. I don't know. I just wasn't given much time for thinking about it. A detective came to me with something that took my mind off it. He'd just had it on the prowl-car radio. They had run down the registration on the station wagon. He had for me the name of the owner and the information that the wagon had not been reported stolen.

Now it was my turn to take off on the run. This was real news and I wasn't waiting for Gibby to come back. I went after him. I found the hamburger joint and Gibby was just coming out of the booth when I hit it. He got to speak first because I was having a little breath trouble. I'd run that hard.

"We were overdue for a break," Gibby said. "I've been talking to the boys down at the phone company. They're throwing out everything that isn't in a beach neighborhood. It comes down to proportions that can be handled —temporarily disconnected telephones in beach houses within the city limits and in nearby suburbs. We know it's near because we know the outside limits of the time he had for getting out there, getting killed, and getting brought back into town."

I had just about given up on that disconnected phone angle. It had looked too hopeless. I could see Gibby's point. It had moved over into distinctly hopeful territory.

"You've got something there, boy," I said, "and it isn't all we've got. The owner of that station wagon is our old friend Hulon Stewart himself. We've had a check on the license number."

Gibby grinned. "That figures," he said. "We did see it parked out in front of his house."

Seven

W E NEVER DID GET any sleep that night. We had a breakfast of sorts, coffee and stuff somebody brought into the local precinct station house. I remember that we poured it into us in intervals between bouts of questioning. The boys were taking Ed and Sam separately and, although the two squirts were talking freely, it just went on and on, steadily more of the same.

That we had them dead to rights on a car-theft charge was obvious, and essentially all their talk came to no more than that. They were admitting the obvious. That in the process they were also confessing to other car thefts could have been read to mean that they were telling the whole truth, but in that area you quickly ran into a heavy atmosphere of doubt. On their own story, they'd been out to steal a car. They had made a most unlucky choice of cars to steal.

It was not an unreasonable story, but it was just their

story; and, when we put pressure on it, they did inevitably cast about for something more they could say, something that would enhance its credibility. What they really needed if they were going to succeed in holding the thing down to this lesser charge was something like a nice, tight alibi for a couple of the earlier hours of the night. That they didn't have.

It is true that at the time we came on the bodies, Dora and Bronson hadn't been long dead but it hadn't been any matter of just minutes. Just on the basis of the surface temperature of the bodies, we could estimate that they had been killed at least an hour before. It wouldn't have been too much earlier than that. It couldn't have been any later.

An alibi that would have started about a half hour after the time Bud Bronson had gone blasting out of the first Mrs. Stewart's apartment and that would run till possibly a half hour before we saw them pull the station wagon out of Sixty-second Street would have been really useful to that pair of kids. If a man is anywhere in midtown Manhattan, there is no place he can go where he will hit a beach that wouldn't involve a minimum of a half hour for getting there.

On the evidence of the sand we knew that much. After leaving Susan Stewart's Bronson had gone somewhere where he had walked on a beach. It was not until after he had walked on that beach that he died and that set the earlier limit on the time of his killing. There was every likelihood that it hadn't been all that early. His body didn't seem cold enough for it. Most of the beach spots around town couldn't be reached in as little as a half hour. So far as we knew, he had gone to Susan

Stewart's with no knowledge of where he might go to find Dora. If we were going to assume that he had found her a half hour after he left there, it would have to have been that in the course of that visit he had picked up his clue. It was either that or it would be that he had come to Susan Stewart's in the course of trying a couple of alternative places. Not having found his Dora there, he had tried at the next place on his list, some place on a beach. He had found her there and he had been killed there.

It was a good bet that they had both been killed at about the same time. That, too, we had on the surface temperatures of the bodies. The one hadn't cooled down noticeably more than the other. That the killings had been done out at the beach place was another good bet. There was, of course, a remote possibility that Bronson had been running down a list of places. He had drawn a blank at Susan Stewart's. He had gone out to the beach and drawn a blank there. He had gone on to a third possibility and there he had found Dora Mason and there they had both been killed.

It was a possibility and, if you have all the time in the world, you can do the thorough sort of job and run down every last possibility. We didn't have all the time in the world. In a kidnaping you never do. You have to ride along with your best bets. There were two elements of the thing that made us accept the beach location as our number-one chance. The total span of time was too short. For Bronson to have made it out to a beach and from there come back into town to look into another possible hideout was just conceivable within the limits of time but everything would have to have happened at top speed.

More conclusive, however, was the other element and that was the quantity of sand Gibby had found stuck to Bronson's shoes. There had been too much of it. If Bronson had been on his feet for any length of time after that beach, he would have shed a lot more of that sand. He would certainly have walked almost all of it off the soles of his shoes and he would have shed a great deal of it out of the indentations between his soles and the uppers.

All these calculations of time, furthermore, were based on the assumption that Bronson had left Susan Stewart's knowing where he was going next. We had no guarantee of that. On the stories we'd had from her and her guests, he had come there seeking information and he had left there no better informed than he'd been on arrival. Had he gone somewhere else afterward where he had picked up his clue? There was considerable likelihood of that and, in that event, the time sequence would be all the tighter.

Taking into account every consideration, the time and place of the killings was pretty well pinpointed, and for that time these kids were offering us nothing in the way of an alibi. There had been a crap game that had broken up about one. They'd hit some bars and grills for about an hour after that. Shortly after two they had cast up accounts on their available funds. The crap game had been a disaster. They had come out of it with only enough on them to cover the round of bars and we gathered that this pub-crawl had been essential. Four or five drinks were what it took to bring their nerve up to the right pitch for car stealing.

They had known all along that they were going to finish up the night stealing a car. That crap game had put them into a position where it was a financial necessity. Shortly after two they had arrived at the decision. They left the last of their bars and started on the long prowl that had finally brought them to what had seemed precisely the right car for their project.

Shortly after two, of course, Bronson had still been alive. It had been later than that when he'd skipped out of Susan Stewart's place. So there it was. For any possible time when Bud Bronson might have been killed these kids had nothing to give us except the story that they had been walking up one street and down another, looking for just that right car to steal.

It was a long time for them to have been occupied that way but they had the readiest of explanations for that. They were old hands at car theft. They had their techniques. They made careful choices. They had behind them successful careers at this game and you don't build a successful career in any branch of larceny by hurrying things.

It was by no means an unbelievable story. The chief thing I could find against it was that it was too much the kind of story a criminal will most typically come up with when he has been caught in the act. It builds an admirable atmosphere of candor by readily admitting all those things which in any case cannot be concealed and then surrounds the necessary admission with just those details which are best calculated to limit guilt to only that which has already been discovered.

We left the boys to the police detectives and we went back around to Sixty-second Street. We hadn't forgotten that we'd promised the Stewarts that we would keep away from them until Hulon Stewart's ten o'clock meeting with the Old Man at the Union League. Circumstances had changed all that. This time we wouldn't be calling about a kidnaping. We would be working on a stolen station wagon and a couple of murders. Earlier evidences of official attention to the Stewarts could have been interpreted by the kidnapers as representing some deviation on the Stewarts' part from their orders to stay away from the police. Now the kidnapers would have to expect that the Stewarts would be hearing from the police.

Mary answered the doorbell, but Stewart was as nervous about visitors as he had been the night before. He was right at Mary's heels and, when he saw us, his face, which had been haggard, was so suffused with anger that quite suddenly it took on a falsely sanguine look.

"I've been trusting you," he stormed. "This is just what you promised you wouldn't do. You wouldn't come here."

"We had to come," Gibby told him. "This time we've heard from the kidnapers. If you're being watched, this visit will look natural. If we didn't come, the kidnapers would get worried. They'd know we had some sort of working arrangement with you. They may even be testing it out, trying to determine just that, whether we do have a working arrangement with you."

"You've heard from them?" Stewart gasped.

He hurried us into the house.

"The ladies?" Gibby asked.

"Mrs. Stewart is still asleep. I gave her some sleeping pills and she was exhausted. She's still asleep."

"And Miss Stewart?"

"She's out."

"Where?"

"The telephone. Those were her instructions. To go and wait for a call at eight this morning." Stewart was hurrying his answers. He had his own question. "You said you heard?"

"We heard," Gibby said curtly. "You own a station wagon?"

"I have a son. You're torturing me, man."

"Sorry. I'm trying to do this quickly. You do own a station wagon?"

"Yes."

"Where do you keep it?"

"Garage." He named the garage and he was about to start on another question or a fresh protest.

Gibby didn't give him the time. He kept the questions firing in steady and hard.

"When did you have it out last?"

"Oh, weeks ago. I can't remember exactly when."

"It should be in the garage now?"

"Yes. We don't use it in town and none of us has gone out of town in the past few weeks."

Mary interrupted. "Begging your pardon, sir," she said. "Miss Emily had it out yesterday."

Stewart was impatient of the interruption. He wanted this talk about the station wagon out of the way.

"Did she?" he said. "I can't imagine why. She has her own convertible."

"It was for the Yorkville House bazaar, sir," Mary told him. "She had a list of things to pick up from various places and take over there. There were some big things like chairs."

"Thank you, Mary," Stewart murmured. He turned back to us. "My daughter used it yesterday," he said. "I didn't know. It's perfectly all right. What are you getting at?"

"She didn't return it to the garage?"

"Very likely not. She'd park it out front and they'd come from the garage and get it."

"We picked it up early this morning with two young squirts in it. They admit they stole it. They say they found it right out front here, unlocked and with the key in the ignition."

"God damn it," Steward exploded. "I'm not going to be bothered with that now. You said you had something about Lonnie. You heard something."

"These two kids weren't alone in the station wagon," Gibby said. "They had Dora Mason and Bronson in the back."

The anger that had been coloring Stewart's face drained away. He went white.

"Lonnie?" He hardly more than mouthed the child's name. He was trying, but for the moment his voice had left him.

"Not the boy," Gibby said gently. "Just Dora Mason and Bronson."

Stewart found his voice. He was angry again. "But

she's told you," he shouted. "She's told you where she took him. You've gotten something out of her."

"Nothing, Mr. Stewart. Dora Mason is dead. She and Bronson. It's their bodies we found in the station wagon."

"Dead," Stewart moaned. "Oh, no."

"Shot," Gibby told him. "Dumped in the back of the station wagon and the bodies covered with a blanket."

"You said there were some kids driving it. You've talked to them?"

"We've just come from talking to them. Their story is that they spotted the station wagon early this morning when it was double parked out front. The doors were unlocked and the key was in the ignition. It was too easy. They just got in and drove it away. The first they knew they had the bodies in the back was when we were chasing them and they looked back at us."

"Where are they? Let me talk to them. I'll get better answers than that."

"Nothing to indicate that they have any better answers," Gibby said. "There could be more to be gained from talking to your daughter."

"She went out for the call," Stewart moaned. "Now I suppose there won't be a call. I suppose this . . ."

He couldn't finish it.

"There will be a call," Gibby said firmly. "We have to look at this rationally. It can have only the one meaning. Somehow, somewhere, Bronson got a clue. He went looking for them and he went playing a lone hand. He found them and he was shot. Dora was also shot but that was a little different. It was at close range and she had blood under her fingernails. That adds up. The killer had to take his eye off her to deal with Bronson. She tried to get the gun away from the killer. It was something like that. We know she struggled with him. He'll show the marks of where she dug her fingernails into him and she shows the mark of a shot fired at very close range—powder burns."

"And my son," Stewart groaned. "This killer—you called him that—this killer still has Lonnie."

"And he still wants half a million dollars," Gibby said. "You must understand this, Mr. Stewart. Why would the bodies be in the station wagon and parked right here out front? They weren't killed in the street in front of your house. They were brought here and left, practically deposited on your doorstep. What would that be for? It would be to let you know beyond the slightest possibility of doubt that you are dealing with a man you can't fool with. Bronson came around and that wasn't in his plan. So Bronson is dead. Dora tried to buck him and she's dead. He still has the baby. He's making that call and he's telling your daughter that now you know what can happen and you'd better not play games with him. That's the message she's going to bring you, Mr. Stewart."

"And I'm to let her go to him after this? How do I know he won't kill her, too, and hand me her body?"

"You can't know it," Gibby told him. "It's a decision you and she will have to make. You can turn us loose to do what we can and I can't promise you that it doesn't involve risk for the child. I can only say that with your child in hands like these, you're up against the worst kind of risk, whatever you do."

"I'm up against a mad dog."

"You may be, and if you are, letting Miss Stewart go to him will be the wrong choice. You can lose both of them."

"There must be something you can do. You, the police."

"There is," Gibby said. "With your co-operation."

"And your daughter's," I added.

"Mr. Stewart, sir," Mary interrupted. She was at the window, looking through the curtains. "Miss Emily's coming. She looks terrible, sir. She looks sick."

We went to the window. Emily Stewart came running down the street from the avenue. Mary hadn't exaggerated. The girl was running unsteadily. She looked as though she might drop at any step. She came up to the house but she didn't come in. She ran on past. She seemed distracted, frantic.

"I'll go get her," Stewart said, squaring his shoulders.

He was obviously bracing himself for what was to come. Anyone could see the girl was in shock. He was going to have to pull himself together and play the man.

"She had the call," Gibby said grimly. "She's looking for the station wagon."

Stewart started out of the room. We went with him.

"Wait for me here," he said. "Please wait for me here. We're being watched. I'm sure we are."

We dropped back and let him go. Watching at the window, we saw them meet. She had come running back and their meeting was right at the front steps. She had forgotten all about appearances and the possibility that they were being watched.

145

"Daddy," she wailed and she fell into her father's arms.

He said nothing. With his arm around her to support her, he helped her up the steps and into the house. She was sobbing wildly, unable to speak. He took her to a sofa and put her down on it. Then he dropped to his knees beside her and comforted her.

"I know," he said. "I know. Tell me, Emmy, tell me what happened."

"It's all my fault," the girl moaned. "My crazy, rotten carelessness. It's all my fault. It was the station wagon, Daddy. That's how he did it, the station wagon."

"I know about the station wagon. What happened?"

"Yesterday. I left it parked. I forgot to lock it and I forgot and left the key in it. I was going to call the garage and tell them to pick it up, but there was one fool thing and another I was doing first and I forgot to call. You know how I do that. I've done it before. Any other time you would have seen it out there when you got home and you would have called the garage or reminded me to, but it had to be this time. I forgot all about it and then, when that call came, of course, I wasn't remembering anything. I didn't even think of it again until now on the telephone he told me."

"What did he tell you?" Gibby asked.

If she realized that it was another voice or if she had noticed that we were there, she gave no sign. She was too frantic to think about that or care.

"He laughed at me. He told me how I made it easy for him. I left the station wagon out there with the key and everything and that's how he got Dora to go with him. He just took it and drove over to the park and found them there. He told her that you had sent him, Daddy, to pick up Lonnie and her and bring them to you. She knew the station wagon and she never thought to doubt him. It was that easy. Even if it had been my convertible, it couldn't have happened. Dora would have insisted on coming back here first with Lonnie's carriage and then she would have known from Mary that you hadn't sent for her. But I had to be careless with the station wagon. Lonnie's carriage was easy, too. Plenty of room for it and it's all my rotten, careless fault."

"You didn't mean to," Stewart mumbled. "And there's no help for that now. What else did he tell you?"

"That man, that Bronson. He found them. That's what he said. Bronson found them. He said he'd killed Bronson and he said that while he was busy with Bronson Dora jumped him and tried to take the gun away from him. He said he killed her, too. He said he put the bodies in the station wagon and brought them back here. He said we should go look in the station wagon and we'll find them, Dora and Bronson. He said he's not taking any fooling around."

"Lonnie?" Stewart asked. "What did he say about Lonnie?"

"He said Lonnie's all right. He said he's taking good care of Lonnie. He said he watched Dora fix the formula for Lonnie's bottle and he knows how. He said Lonnie will be all right but we have to play it straight with him. One more goof—that's what he called it—one more goof and he'll kill Lonnie. He said it was up to us. He thought we'd sent Bronson."

"Did you tell him?"

"I talked and talked. I think I convinced him. I told him everything. I told him how Bronson came and how Bronson knew and how he brought these people from the District Attorney. I told him how they found out and I swore to him that I didn't tell them where I was going to get his calls. I swore to him that we were following his instructions to the letter. I think I proved it to him. I asked him how he could have driven up to the house in the station wagon and left it parked out front the way he said he did. I asked him how he could have gotten away with that, if we'd had the police in. I showed him how that proved that we didn't have the police watching. He said he left it right out front double parked, but it isn't there. It isn't anywhere in the street. I looked."

"We have it," Gibby said.

She turned and looked at us. It might have been the first she realized we were there.

"You?" she moaned. "Just after I'd told him that it proved you weren't around. Oh, no."

"He left it the way you did," Gibby said. "Doors unlocked, key in the ignition. That's an invitation and the invitation was accepted again. Two punks stole it, bodies and all. We have the lot, station wagon, punks, and bodies."

"Then it is true?" she said. "He did kill them?"

"Bronson and the girl and about the way he told you. The girl he shot at close range and after a struggle. She clawed him some. There's the blood under her fingernails."

"And we have nothing but his word for it that he hasn't harmed Lonnie," Stewart said.

"That's what I said to him," Emily told him. "I asked him what assurances we had that he hasn't harmed Lonnie. I asked him what guarantee he could give me that he would do as he says, give me Lonnie back unhurt tomorrow. He said he hasn't harmed Lonnie and he won't unless we make him do it. He said that if Bronson told the police where he was going and if they come after him, he will kill Lonnie because then Lonnie won't be any good to him any more and he'll have to think about nothing but getting away. He said that even if he wanted to give us a break then, he couldn't because he couldn't let himself be encumbered with a baby. He gave me the formula for Lonnie's bottles to prove that he was taking care of him."

"Did he have it right?" Gibby asked.

"It sounded right. I really don't know. I never fixed a bottle or saw one fixed but it sounded right."

"What was it, Miss?" Mary asked. "Do you remember it?"

"I remember every word he said to me."

She repeated the formula for Mary. So much whole milk, so much water, so much sugar.

Mary nodded. "He's got it right," she said.

"He was on the phone with you a long time," Gibby said.

"Yes. When he first told me, I got hysterical. He had to talk to me and talk to me before I was even able to listen and understand anything. He was very patient with me."

"That," Gibby said dryly, "was nice of him. It could have been very nice if you'd let us know on what phone you receive his calls. Talking that long, he would have given us more than enough time for tracing the call. We could have had him before you were off the phone."

"And Lonnie," the girl said, "would be dead. That's exactly why nobody has known and nobody is going to know."

Gibby made the big try. "Let's reason this thing out," he said. "He can't be telephoning from the place where he's keeping the boy. The telephone he has there has been disconnected. He told you that. He will leave you and the child locked up with the disconnected phone and you won't be able to call out to tell us where you are until the service on that phone opens up again. By that time he'll be gone beyond any hope of our catching up with him."

"He'll have it temporarily disconnected before he leaves me there," Emily argued. "He never said it's already disconnected."

"Em," her father put in. "You're not going, Emmy. That's out. I can't let you go."

"You must, Daddy. Now more than ever you must."

Gibby broke in on her to get the thing back where he wanted it.

"That," he said, "can turn out to be a purely academic argument. If I can make you understand this, Miss Stewart, you'll agree that there is no need for you to go to this man. In fact, there will be no point to doing it."

"You'll never convince me of that," the girl said stubbornly. "You couldn't convince me last night and then I never had the first thought that it could have been my fault. Now that I know it was my fault, all my rotten, crazy carelessness leaving the station wagon that way, do you think anybody's going to take away from me the one chance I have to make this all right? Lonnie's my brother. I have to live with my father. I have to live with myself. Do you think I ever could again if anything happens to Lonnie?"

"Your father," Gibby said, "also has to live with himself. How is he going to manage that if he lets you go and anything happens to both of you—you and your brother?"

"He will have nothing to blame himself for."

"No," Stewart protested. "You're talking like a child."

"I'm no child, Daddy. I know what I'm saying. The choice is mine and only mine and the decision is mine and only mine. That is just as it should be because the fault is also only mine. Nobody else as good as handed this man the station wagon. I did that. It's all my fault."

"No," her father insisted. "This is a decision I have to make. That's out. You won't be going tomorrow."

"And we'll never see Lonnie again, not alive anyhow."

Stewart winced away from the words but he made himself take them.

"I have to choose my risks," he said. "I'm choosing to put it in the hands of these gentlemen and the police. That girl, Dora, is on my conscience already and the man, too, even the man. I can't take any more."

"It's not your choice, Daddy," the girl said firmly. "Either I go to take the next call or that will be it. We'll

151

never hear from him again. He'll know that he's failed. He'll kill Lonnie and he'll disappear."

"We'll do what the men from the District Attorney's office tell us to do," Stewart said. "These gentlemen have been right about this from the first. If we had co-operated with them, the man Bronson would not have gone off that way on his own. Whatever he learned, we would have learned it, too. He and Dora would be alive now and we'd have had Lonnie home and safe. I was wrong last night, Em, and I'm paying an awful price for my mistake."

"You weren't wrong," she cried. "Dora's dead and Bronson is dead and that's terrible. I feel as awful about that as you do, but he told me right out. He killed them because they interfered. He didn't touch Lonnie because he still had a possibility of making his scheme work. At the first sign he sees that he hasn't a possibility, he'll kill Lonnie and he'll get away. He's even thought of the possibility that he won't be able to get away. He told me about that, too. He'll kill Lonnie and he'll kill himself. The police won't take him, not alive, and he'll kill Lonnie first."

"And you as well, Miss Stewart?" Gibby asked.

"Only if there is interference. I won't be a fool like Dora. I won't struggle with him. I won't fight a man with a gun. Nothing can go wrong unless you or my father or the police make it go wrong."

"You still trust this man?"

"I've talked to him. I'm the only one who's talked to him and I have to trust my judgment. I don't fool myself about him. He's determined and he's ruthless, but he's practical. God, he's practical. And there's another thing. He's vain. He's planned this from beginning to end beautifully and he's proud of the way he's planned it. He wants the money, of course, but there's that pride too. He wants his plan to work out. He wants to commit the perfect crime and in kidnaping it is perfection to return the child unharmed and get away with the ransom. We can let him have that, Daddy. It's worth it to have Lonnie back alive."

"That," Gibby said softly, "is worth anything and everything. You're right about your man. He is vain. He's a long way off from having planned the perfect crime. I was drawing the picture for you. He goes out to telephone you because he can't use the phone in his hideout. He's had that disconnected in preparation for locking you up there tomorrow."

"You said that before and I told you that he'll have it disconnected tomorrow. I told you that he never said it's already been disconnected."

"We know it has."

"How can you know?"

"Very simply," Gibby said. "This perfect plan was so imperfect that he didn't foresee that Saturday afternoon was the worst sort of timing for the quick snatch, the quick ransom payment, and the quick getaway. He goofed right there. He should have picked a time when the banks would be open and your father could have made an immediate start on raising the ransom money."

"No, he didn't," the girl said quickly. "He needed the station wagon. He needed that so he could get Dora to go with him. He had to move when he had the opportunity, when I left the station wagon unlocked and with the key in it. He had plenty of those opportunities. I've always been careless about that, but it had to be at a time when Dora was in the park with Lonnie and it had to be the station wagon because of Lonnie's carriage. It couldn't be late at night or any other time because then, by the time he would have a chance at Dora and Lonnie, we'd have known that the car had been stolen and obviously Dora couldn't be persuaded to go off with a stranger in one of our cars when she knew that it had been stolen."

"How do you know that controlled his timing?" Gibby asked.

"He told me so. He told me it was too bad I didn't leave the station wagon in the street for him some other day of the week, a day when the banks would have been open the very next morning and we wouldn't have had to go through this long an ordeal. He told me that to show me that I could trust him because none of this was sadistic. There wasn't any of it that wasn't absolutely necessary."

"Okay," Gibby conceded. "Then he didn't goof on that part of it and that makes it even more certain that he hasn't goofed on the telephone either. He had the phone disconnected before the kidnaping. The company will not do one of these temporary disconnecting deals for any period less than fifteen days. Do you expect that he'll have it disconnected Monday and leave you locked up there to wait fifteen days before you can make a call out of there?"

"All right," the girl said impatiently. "Then it's been

disconnected. He goes out to telephone me. What difference does that make?"

"All the difference in the world. If we had been in on this during any one of those long conversations you've been having with this goon, this would have been all over right then. Let us in on the next one and that will do it. We spot the phone he's calling from. We get plenty of men over there and we nab him while he's still talking. He can't do anything to the child because he has to go out to make these calls and he can't get back to the child to harm it. That's obvious. That's simple. Once we have him, he'll tell us where he has the boy. He'll be in for murder and kidnaping anyhow. He'll know he hasn't a prayer with any jury. The only glimmer he'll have left then is a chance of clemency and there won't be even that glimmer if he keeps us waiting as much as a minute before he tells us where to go to find your brother. There's nothing tricky about this, Miss Stewart. I'm not trying to pull any fast ones on you. That is the way these things work."

"Except that this one doesn't work that way. I can see you're right about one thing. He does go out to make the calls. He has to since the phone has to have been already disconnected. But you're wrong about the rest of it. He doesn't go out and leave Lonnie behind. He takes Lonnie with him. He has Lonnie right there with him all the time he's talking to me. On every one of the calls I've heard Lonnie. I've heard him cry. He stops talking for a while and he lets me hear Lonnie. He tells me to listen so I'll know that he has Lonnie right there with him and I'll know that Lonnie will be right there all the time, right where he can kill the poor baby if anything goes wrong."

"He's told you that?"

"Of course he has. Why do you suppose I've been so stubborn about this? I can't let anything go wrong. I can't. I can't."

Eight

AND THERE IT WAS. We'd had it. We came away from there that Sunday morning no further along than we'd been when we came in. All the change we had was for the worse. We hadn't persuaded Emily Stewart and we'd lost Hulon Stewart. Oh, it was a struggle. It was a ding-dong battle all the way for the mind of Hulon Stewart; but, when it was over, we couldn't kid ourselves. We'd lost and Emily Stewart had won.

Even that small bit we'd managed the night before went down the drain. That meeting at the Union League with the Old Man—Hulon Stewart called it off. We were out. We were finished. We were through. It was to be completely hands off until we'd had the word from him and he left us in no doubt about when we would have the word. That would come not when he might want it or when we might want it. It would come not one minute earlier than when the kidnaper wanted it.

Emily would keep the contacts going and, if she was followed or watched when she went to take a call, she would not go. She told us that even that contingency had been provided for. If he called and she wasn't there to take it, he would call again in an hour and again in another hour or on some such schedule. She wouldn't, of course, trust us so far that she would give us the exact timing on it. He would continue calling until she was there except, of course, for the possibility that, if he was disappointed too many times, he might give up on it. He might kill the child and take off, but he had instructed her on that point as on all others. She was not to go and take a call unless she was certain that she was going unobserved. The first time she was followed when she went to take a call and she didn't turn back and wait till the next appointed hour, he would know that she was double-crossing him and the baby would be killed.

Monday morning Hulon Stewart would go out and raise the ransom money. He would bring it home and on the next contact after that, when she could tell the kidnaper that the ransom was ready, she would have her instructions for delivering it. She would go and she was not to be followed. If she was followed, she was to turn back and go to the phone for further instructions. She would go alone and she would deliver the ransom. She would submit completely to the kidnaper's terms. She would wait, locked up with the baby, till the telephone was connected again. At that point she wasn't going to call us. She was going to call her father. He would go and get her. He would bring her and Lonnie home. Only then and not before then would we hear from him, when he had them home and knew they were safe.

At that magic moment we would have complete co-operation. We had not only Hulon Stewart's promise of that. We had his daughter's as well. We would be taken to the hideout. We would be free to examine it for fingerprints or for anything else we might find toward tracking this kidnaper down. We would have a complete report from Emily Stewart on everything she knew, what the man looked like, what sort of voice he had, how he was dressed, a complete description. At that point he would be ours and all we'd have to do was search the whole damn world for him.

This was total defeat. It was just about as total as you can come up with on any job of law enforcement. It was Emily, of course, who hit us first. She laid it on the line. She couldn't have been franker with us. She recognized that two people had been murdered and that the State didn't have to wait for anyone to come in and make a complaint before we could move in a matter of murder. We had the bodies, and nobody could stop us from making an investigation of the deaths of Dora Mason and Lawrence Bronson.

She couldn't stop us but she was asking us. She was begging. It was the life of Little Lonnie and that was all she wanted of us. We were to let them get Lonnie home safely and we weren't to louse that up by making even the first move toward finding the killer of Dora Mason and Bud Bronson. All that was to wait till after she had secured the safety of her baby brother.

We worked at trying to show her that we had safer

ways than this way of hers, but it was no dice all down the line. I've given you the story on the idea of catching this goon at the phone and making him take us back to the baby. We had Stewart going beautifully on that one and then with a word she fractured it. He did take the baby with him when he went to the telephone. He let her hear the baby cry every time.

With each try we made, it got worse because on each one she had the same answer for us. The kidnaper had foreseen that move. He'd told her how he was prepared to handle it. You can see how the picture built. No matter how screwily dangerous it might seem to play along with this man and hew straight to the line on all his directions without even allowing us and the police to know what was being done, it still seemed more dangerous to do anything else. You could see how it had convinced her. You can see how it would convince her old man.

There was only one thing that had him hanging back at all and that was his natural unwillingness to consent to letting her risk her neck on the ransom contact. He didn't like that, of course, and nothing could make him like it, but he was stymied. The girl was determined to do it and at any point where it came to a showdown she was immovable. We would have nothing from her and he would have nothing from her. She had to do it. The kidnaper would deal with no one but her, and he wouldn't deal even with her unless she was playing the completely lone hand. It was that or nothing.

Once she had her old man convinced of it, we were down the drain. He was right in there with her. We were to do nothing because our slightest move would be jeopardizing not only his son's safety but his daughter's as well. We could quote the law at him till we ran out of breath. He wasn't arguing law. He was arguing humanity.

"Look," he said. "I'm telling you this and I mean it. You have the two bodies. You have the station wagon. You have those boys you say you picked up driving it. You've got the murders to investigate. I don't care how you investigate them. Any clues you can get from the bodies, get them. Anything you can get out of those boys, get it. That's all right, but you have to stop there. Even if you find out exactly where this man is, where he has my little boy, you mustn't go near him. You mustn't touch him. You must stay away from it completely until I tell you that I have my son back and my daughter back and you can move without jeopardizing their safety."

"Mr. Stewart," Gibby said, "we can't do that."

"Nobody can do it," I added. "We've taken an oath to uphold the law. That means something."

"I know what it means," Stewart shouted, "and I know that nobody is going to uphold any law at the cost of the lives of my children. You make one move and I'll protect myself with the only way that's open to me. I'll call in the newspapers and I'll give them the whole story. They'll print what I'll give them. They'll print my assurances to the kidnaper that I want my baby back so much that I want him to have the five hundred thousand dollars. I want him to get it and I want him to get away with it and I want him to live in immunity for the rest of his life and enjoy it. That's how much I want that child back. I'll lay it on the line in the newspapers and all over the radio and television. I'll leave it to public opinion. If anything happens to my son, the public will be your judge. It's going to be right out there in black and white. I'm not going to the Union League. I'm not going to meet the District Attorney. I have nothing to say to him. I have nothing to say to any of you except that, and you can take him my message. Hulon Stewart doesn't give a damn for the law. He doesn't give a damn for anything except getting his son back safe and unharmed. Dora Mason is dead. Bronson is dead. Nothing you can do will bring them back. Watch out you don't do something that kills my boy."

"It isn't that simple, Mr. Stewart," I began.

He didn't wait for me to finish.

"To me it is exactly that simple," he said.

"Not even to you," Gibby said firmly. "You want your boy back so much that you want the kidnaper to have the money, you want him to get clean away, and you want him to enjoy that half million dollars the rest of his life in complete immunity. You want that child back so much that you want to make kidnaping a safe and foolproof and attractive crime. You want to make it so attractive that neither your child nor any other child in this country will ever be safe again. You want to make it so attractive that you'll never be able to let that child out again unless he's surrounded by an armed guard. Is that what you want, Mr. Stewart?"

"For now it's what I want," he answered. "It's first things first and you won't find a father who could want anything else."

"All right," Gibby said. "We'll take your message to

the District Attorney. We take our orders from him. We'll let you know what he says."

"Do that, but it's hands off. It has to be. I want my boy back."

We were licked in that quarter and it was no good fighting it further. We moved to pull out. In the hall we ran into Gloria Stewart, Little Lonnie's mother. If it hadn't been for the shape, I don't think I would have known her. Maybe nobody would have known her. We, of course, had never seen Gloria at her best. We'd seen her only that once the night before when she had been as she had probably never been otherwise. Now she was as different as she could be, but again it was probably as she had never been otherwise. She was wearing a black sweater and a gray skirt and, as I said, there was the shape and you could recognize her by that. Otherwise it was all white face and pale lips, haggard eyes and pale hair. The hair was drawn smoothly back from her face and done up neatly and tightly on the back of her head.

No lipstick, no mascara, no eyeshadow, no make-up of any kind, not even a little dab of powder. She looked like a pretty little girl, a little girl who had grown up overnight and had grown sad overnight and had broken her heart overnight.

"I have been out here," she said. "I've been listening. It's been years since I've been to church. I don't even remember how many years it's been. I'm going now. I'm going to church and I'm going to pray, because I've been listening and now I know how good people can be. My husband and Emily—I've been listening to them and I'm ashamed. I know now how I've been sinning against them. Even in what I've been thinking, that was sinning. Thinking that Emily didn't want me here. Thinking that she didn't want Lonnie, that she was jealous of me and the baby. Thinking that my husband was worrying about the money. All that. If Lonnie doesn't come back to us, if he isn't all right, it will be a punishment on me. I know that now. I'm going to church and I'm going to ask God not to punish me or I'm going to ask him to punish me any way he likes but not through my baby. My husband and Emily are doing everything that humans can do. There isn't anything I can do except pray and I'm going to do that. There isn't anything you can do but go away and forget us. Please do that. Go away and forget us. Don't hurt my baby, please."

"You have nothing to fear from us, Mrs. Stewart," I said.

"You promise?"

"You've never had anything to fear from us," Gibby said. "We'll promise you that."

"You'll go away and forget us?"

"I don't think we can do that, Mrs. Stewart."

She dropped to her knees and she grabbed at us. She caught us both around the legs with her arms and she hung there, kneeling to us and begging. We had to reach down and loosen her hands and pull ourselves away from her, and she followed us all the way to the front door, shuffling after us on her knees and begging and begging.

When we finally got out of there, I was ready to quit. There was nothing in the world I wanted to do except go straight up to the Old Man's place and hand him my resignation as of right that minute. To hell with making the big career, I was thinking. To hell with all those dreams of being on the bench one day. Why aren't you out of this and into private practice? Ambulance chasing —that's a living and it's better than this.

I said a little of it to Gibby and that got him on to telling me what he thought of me. We don't have to go through all of that. Soft and yellow were the least of it. The most of what he said can remain between Gibby and me. Each of us has his own way of handling his feelings.

We did get together with the Old Man. That was mandatory. In the first place, he had to be told that Hulon Stewart was not coming to meet with him and why and, in the even more important second place, he had to be brought up to date on Hulon Stewart's ultimatum and the threat that accompanied it. You have to remember that District Attorney is an elective office. You can't have a DA that isn't also a politician and that's a ticklish business. Come election time, a man doesn't want the record to turn up any dereliction of duty. Equally, however, one doesn't want it to turn up any clumsy fumbling.

In any job of crime detection or law enforcement thousands of things can go wrong. When you are dealing with kidnaping, however, the things that go wrong can do so most horribly and this was a setup in which we, the DA's office and the police, would obviously be taking the full blame for anything that went wrong. The Stewarts could make every mistake in the book and the worst that anyone would say of them would be that grief and terror may have warped their judgment. We didn't have to make any mistakes at all. If we did anything less than bring off a miracle, we were going to be resoundingly wrong.

We'd already lost Dora Mason and Bud Bronson and we couldn't lose any more. Little Lonnie Stewart had to come out of this safely. Emily Stewart had to come out of it safely. And that wasn't all that would be required of us. We also would be expected to nab the kidnaper or kidnapers and save Hulon Stewart every last buck of that huge ransom money. Anything less than that and we were dead ducks.

There was a council of war. The Old Man was in on it and the Police Commissioner and that was to have been expected, but we also had the Mayor. Gibby made the big pitch to them as he had to Stewart. Holding off till the ransom had been paid and the kid returned was impossible. Even if there had been no murder in this thing, it would have been bad, an open invitation to goons anywhere to come into town and have a try at kidnaping. But there was murder. Two people had been killed. Two bodies had been thrown in our faces. We couldn't sit back and wait till the killer was ready to tell us that now it was okay. Now we could start doing our job. Now we could start looking for him.

Both the Old Man and the Police Commissioner were ready to string along with us. They weren't happy about it, but everybody knows what Gilbert said about a policeman's lot. It goes for DAs, too. It was with the Mayor that we ran into real trouble. The Mayor just didn't want anybody to take any risks. He saw the thing as Emily Stewart saw it. Do just as the kidnaper ordered and that would be playing it safe.

"And he gets away," Gibby said.

"He won't get away," said the Mayor, laying on his best I-have-every-confidence-in-you-boys manner.

"He gives himself exactly as much head start as he wants," the Old Man argued. "Twenty-four hours, maybe forty-eight. He'll take a lot of finding after that. You can lose them even when they haven't had that much head start."

"We can plaster the whole world with circulars," the Mayor said glibly. "We'll have Miss Stewart's description of the man and we'll have the serial numbers of the bills in the ransom money. You've picked up people with far less to go on than that."

"Assuming that he gives us that much," Gibby said.

The Mayor was assuming it. He was even assuming that Hulon Stewart would co-operate to the extent of getting us a record of those serial numbers.

"That," Gibby reminded him, "is in the kidnaper's instructions. No record of serial numbers on the bills."

"Now, come," the Mayor said. "We're dealing with a man. He's clever and he's ruthless, but he hasn't supernatural powers. If Miss Stewart is watched when she takes his calls, he may have a way of knowing that. If she is followed when she goes to bring him the ransom money, he may have a way of knowing that. He can't possibly have any way of knowing whether a record of those serial numbers is made or not."

"He has a way of knowing that Hulon Stewart can be scared enough to make him follow the instructions to the letter, even to that much of a letter. He's got the man's son. He's demanding that the man's daughter also be delivered into his hands. He's taking as hostages everything Hulon Stewart has and he's convinced Emily Stewart that he's Superman. She's put it up to her father. She has the courage to go to this man, bring him the money, let him lock her up with that baby for whatever length of time he sees fit. She has the courage for all that but only if she goes knowing that this man is being given every last thing he's asked for. Anything that's done, no matter how safe, is going to break her down. It won't be that she won't still want to save the kid, but she'll be convinced that we've fixed it so that there won't be any kid to save."

"She needn't know," the Mayor said, but now he was a little less glib about it. "We can set it up with Hulon Stewart. It will be better if the girl doesn't know. It will be better if she believes we've withdrawn completely."

I held my breath. I knew Gibby well enough to guess what would be coming next and it was going to be something that no Assistant DA ever allows himself to say to the Mayor, not under any circumstances. The Old Man, fortunately, also knows Gibby. He took over.

"It won't work, Mr. Mayor. You have a daughter. Try putting yourself in Stewart's place. It's not going to be easy, letting her go to this man. When a father has been pushed far enough to be ready to do what he is going to do, you can't expect that you'll be able to reason with him. Gibby and Mac here have been trying to make him see that if he lets us work with him on this thing, the chance of saving his son is better and that, with our help, he might forestall any danger to his daughter. Even with those stakes in the pot, he's switched away from us. He believes that his best chance lies in going along completely with this kidnaper's instructions. Sure, after it's all over, after he has his kids home safely, he'll be expecting us to catch the kidnaper and get his half million back for him, but that will be afterward.

"When he puts the money into that girl's hands and lets her go off, he's going to be too scared to make any sense. You can tell him from here to Christmas that he can keep a record of the serial numbers and there can be no way for the kidnaper to know it, but he won't see it that way. His way is going to be that the girl is going out to do this terrific thing for him. It's going to be that he doesn't know whether he's doing right in letting her go at all. It's going to be that, since he is letting her go, he can't do anything but be completely honest with her. At that point, Mr. Mayor, we're going to be up against a superstitious kind of fear. He won't send the girl out on an errand like that with the knowledge that he's lying to her. You wouldn't. I wouldn't. You can't expect that he will."

There was a lot more of that with all of us pitching in and finally the Mayor conceded the point. He was still ready to settle for half the assets.

"We'll still have Miss Stewart's description of the man," he said, and then he worked at building it up. "We'll have a lot more than that," he added. "There will be fingerprints. There will be all kinds of clues he'll have left around the hideout. No matter how smart and how careful he is, he'll be leaving us all kinds of stuff we can work on. There has to be something he'll miss out on, particularly since he has this all planned in a way that has him banking on this head start he's going to have. His eye will be on that and on covering his trail after he leaves Miss Stewart. He won't be thinking too much of what he leaves us in the house or wherever it is that he's keeping the child."

The Police Commissioner stepped in to knock that one down. "I don't know," he said. "We've been working on the station wagon and the bodies. He picked up the bodies and loaded them into the car and he drove the car back around to Stewart's to leave it there. He didn't leave us one fingerprint or anything else. We've got prints on the car but they all belong to those two punks we're holding. We can't count on his leaving us much. We had hopes with the blanket, but now that's like the rest. It's Stewart's. It was in the station wagon when the man stole it."

"Now wait a minute," the Mayor argued. "There is the sand on Bronson's shoes and the sand in the cuffs of Bronson's pants. He left us that and leaving us that was mighty careless. It's not as though it was only a couple of grains embedded in the cloth. It wasn't something turned up in your police laboratories. It was so conspicuous that these boys here turned it up out in the street on only a cursory examination. He's going to leave us plenty."

"He will, Mr. Mayor," Gibby said, "and he won't. He's built his whole plan on one thing. He's built it on scaring the Stewarts to the point where they'll do nothing but play along. He's built it on convincing Emily Stewart that playing along is their only chance. He had a good scheme there and it was only an unforeseeable contingency that spoiled it. He didn't know that Bronson would be coming around to help Dora Mason with her Saturday night baby-sitting."

"The way he researched those people," the Police Commissioner murmured, "you'd think he would have known that, as well."

"He may very well have known it, sir," Gibby said. "He knows so much that he has the Stewarts believing that he can also know the unknowable, but we can take a cooler view of it. He builds an atmosphere where he has you feeling that he's looking over your shoulder all the time, that somehow he's seeing and hearing everything you do and say. More than that, he makes you feel as though he even knows what you're thinking. He might have known that Bronson would be coming around to spend the evening with Dora. But he couldn't know that when Bronson was told she was out he would follow up on it the way he did."

The Mayor sighed. "I wish we had some way of knowing how Bronson did follow up on it," he said. "There's no indication that he knew anything more than you knew and still he found the man and you didn't even know where to begin looking."

He didn't quite say it, but the implication was there. He was wishing law enforcement people could be as competent as crooks.

"Bronson," Gibby said, "fell into some kind of a crazy break. I wish we knew what it was. We do know it was nothing that could have been foreseen. Bronson himself didn't foresee it. He would never have come to us if he had. But I'm not talking about Bronson's finding him. I'm talking about Bronson's going into the house, hearing enough to know it was a snatch, coming to us with it. The kidnaper couldn't and didn't foresee that. He made his pitch to Emily Stewart. He convinced her that she and her father and her stepmother couldn't so much as move a finger without his knowing it. He convinced her that he would even know what they were thinking. Until Bronson brought us into the picture, everything was going exactly as the kidnaper had planned it. Except for Bronson, it would have gone right down to the end the way that kidnaper wanted it. The child would never have been reported missing. Emily Stewart would have gone to him with the ransom money. Her father would have waited for her to telephone him. Twenty-four hours, forty-eight hours, whatever time the girl had told him it was going to be. Then there would have been no call. Maybe Stewart would have given it more time. Maybe he would have come to us then. Either way he would have come to us eventually and eventually, depending on how lucky or unlucky we were, we would have found the three bodies—Dora Mason's, Emily Stewart's, and the baby's."

The Mayor swallowed hard. "Gibson," he said, "is that what you meant when you said he will leave us plenty and he won't? You meant that, in your opinion, he won't leave Miss Stewart or the baby? He'll kill them?"

"He may leave the baby," Gibby said, "and if we're lucky and we find it quickly enough, we might save that much. I don't know how long you can expect an infant to live locked up some place with nobody to feed it or take care of it. He won't leave us Emily Stewart and he wouldn't have left us Dora Mason. Because Bronson turned up, he had to kill Dora earlier than he planned; but let's not kid ourselves about this man. He's too ruthless, too cold-blooded, and too smart. He won't leave us anyone who can give us a description of him."

"You've told the Stewarts that?" the Mayor asked.

"No," Gibby exploded. "That's the last thing we can do. They're so scared now that they aren't much good to themselves or us. Scare them any more and they'll be no good at all."

The Mayor scowled. "I don't for one moment agree that we can let them go unwarned. They must at least have this possibility presented to them. They must be allowed to consider it."

"They have considered it," Gibby said. "I haven't told them that it is a certainty. At the beginning I brought it in as a possibility. That's how I got Stewart to agree to meet the DA. Miss Stewart will not consider it even as a possibility. She is absolutely convinced that going along completely according to the instructions she gets on the phone is the only safe method. She's convinced her father. I can give him the argument I've just given you and I can unconvince him. That won't do us any good."

"It will persuade him to co-operate, Gibby," the Old Man said. There was more hope in his voice than conviction.

Gibby knocked down the hope. "Nothing," he said, "is going to persuade the girl to co-operate. She's got the full deal going. It was her fault and she's got to risk her neck to compensate. She *wants* to put herself into danger. She's making a kind of religious necessity of it. Sure. If she would keep the contacts going, play along, and keep us posted on every detail, I am confident that we could do something with this guy. He's making every kind of mistake. He's going out to make these long phone calls and he's taking the baby with him. A guy shuts himself up in a phone booth with a baby in his arms and talks as long as he does, he's making himself crazily conspicuous. He sent Bronson back with sand on his shoes. He's made more than his share of mistakes. We should have had a dozen chances at him in the last twelve hours and we should have a dozen more in the next twelve, but the one thing we're not going to have is the co-operation of Emily Stewart, and that's where he's got us on the hip.''

"Now wait a minute," the Mayor said. "This can be handled. We don't have to convince the girl. We convince her father. You agree that it's possible to convince him. Once he's convinced, he'll refuse to give her the ransom money to take to that man on that man's terms. She'll have to co-operate then.''

"No, she won't," Gibby said. "I know exactly what she'll do then. She'll make the next phone contact as always. She'll tell the kidnaper exactly what the score is and she'll beg him to set it up some other way. She'll promise him immunity and all that and he'll turn her down flat. He's that smart. He has to be. Then what happens?''

"They return to the original plan," the Mayor said.

"We'll be no worse off than we are now. We'll at least have tried."

"We'll be no worse off if the kidnaper is patient enough," Gibby said. "Suppose he takes it to mean that there's too much police in the thing and his plan isn't any good any more. Suppose he decides to say goodbye to the ransom money and save his own skin. Suppose he kills the child and takes off."

"And if his instructions are followed to the letter, Gibby," the DA put in, "you're expecting him to kill the Stewart girl and leave the child to die of neglect. Is that good?"

"Not if Mac and I have our way," Gibby said.

"What's your way, Gibson?" the Mayor asked.

Then Gibby made his pitch. He would tell the Stewarts they had won. We would tell them that we were keeping hands off, that we were waiting till they gave us the word before we made any move at all. We would let them go ahead in the belief that we were out of the picture entirely.

"We keep away from them," he said. "Just in case this guy's intelligence is as good as Emily Stewart seems to think it is. We work every other angle we have, the sand, a man who shuts himself up in telephone booths with a baby in his arms, Bronson. We put everything we've got into trying to pick up Bronson's trail from the time he left the first Mrs. Stewart's apartment. We continue the sifting of the temporarily disconnected telephone numbers. We have twenty-four hours. This time tomorrow Stewart will be hitting the banks. Some time after that Emily Stewart will go to pay the ransom. If we don't have him before then, we'll have to take the chance on tailing her when she goes. With enough luck we may not have to take that chance."

"If we do take the chance," the Mayor moaned, "and anything goes wrong, we'll have the devil's own time justifying ourselves."

"I'd rather we got lucky before that," Gibby said. "I'd like to try."

Considering how little time we had and the proportions of the needle-in-the-haystack operation that lay ahead of us, it was rough having to use up so much of that time talking the Mayor into letting the DA turn us loose on it, but it had to be done. It did take time and, even when we finally were turned loose, it was done grudgingly. A whole flock of political futures were at stake.

Eventually, however, we were out of there. The first move was made from right there at the conference. An order went out to all precincts. We were looking for a man who was making calls from telephone booths. He had made several calls which were of considerable duration and he always had with him for these sessions in the telephone booth a small infant. This infant, furthermore, could be expected to do some crying while the man was on the phone. He would be making further calls and he would probably again have the infant with him. He might also be showing some fresh scratches on his face or possibly on his hands.

If spotted, he was to be trailed most discreetly and the report was to come to us directly. He was not to be touched, only kept under observation and that only to the extent that it could be done safely. We wanted it understood by all personnel that it would be better to lose the man than to risk his noticing that he was under observation.

By the time the whole of that order had gone out, I was wondering whether it would even be worth the bother. With the Mayor and the Old Man breathing down our necks, we'd been forced to wrap it around with so many cautions and reservations that it amounted to little more than telling police officers all over town that it would be nice if they happened to spot this guy and even nicer if he happened to be so unwary that he could be trailed to his lair without his noticing it; but, that if they preferred to sit on their fat tails and not exert themselves, they had the perfect out. They could report spotting him and losing him and there would be no more explanation required of them than the simple statement that he looked as though he might turn his head.

Getting away from the huddle, I was grumbling about it. Gibby, unexpectedly, was far more cheerful.

"It doesn't matter," he said. "I know cops. Sure, it's an easy out for the slobs; but the slobs are slobs and, if you don't give them an easy out, they find one for themselves. Good cops don't look for outs. Hand them an easy out and they won't take it."

"How many cops are there who are that good?"

"More than you think, Mac, more than you think and, many or few, it doesn't matter either. If you think there's any order you can toss out that will get you effective action from anybody but the good cops on the force, you've suddenly gone naïve on me. It comes to the same thing, however you do it. The good boys will be in there working for you. The slobs remain slobs."

We hit it first at police headquarters. We looked at everything they had and it added up to everything we'd already had and nothing noticeably more. Both Dora and Bronson had been shot. It had taken two shots for Bronson and only one for Dora. Dora had been shot at close range with the gun muzzle all but touching her body. The two bullets had been taken out of Bronson and the one out of Dora. All were .32s. All had been fired from the same gun.

The slug that killed Dora had entered her upper abdomen and had plowed an upward course to find her heart. It had been largely because of that angle that the slug had remained in her body. A less oblique shot at that close range would have gone right through her and we would have had for it a point of entry and a point of exit. Before she died Dora had drawn blood with her fingernails. What we had seen embedded under them was just what it looked like and a little more. It was blood and fragments of skin and a little of something else. That little of something else was a dark-toned theatrical make-up.

"A character who likes to look suntanned even when he isn't," I said disgustedly, "or one who's done what he can to change his appearance in the hope that it will throw off any descriptions of him we'll be picking up. That's going to be a big help."

"It's something," Gibby said brightly. "It tells us that

he's light-skinned. The ones with dark complexions don't try to change their appearance with dark make-up."

"All right," I growled. "If you like it that much, add it to the description. Light-skinned man wearing scratches and dark make-up who takes a baby into telephone booths and stays in there holding long conversations which include intermissions for the baby's crying into the phone."

"Not worth adding," Gibby said. "We can figure he's smart enough to do a good enough make-up job so that he looks dark and not like a paleface wearing dark paint."

"Exactly what I mean," I said. "What good does it do us?"

"It's information," Gibby said, "and we haven't so much that every little bit won't help."

On at least half of that I was ready to agree with him. We didn't have much. The lab boys had also worked at a stain on the front of the left shoulder of Dora's uniform. They'd analyzed it and they could tell us it was milk and Pablum. That was a big deal. Ask anyone who's ever had anything to do with feeding a baby. After the kid's finished you hold it up to burp it. Unless you're both careful and lucky, when the burp comes, you get squirted a bit in just that spot.

It set me to thinking about what the boys had been saying about the good cops and the slobs. The boys in the police labs are good cops. They go after everything whether the results are rewarding or not. They'd been after that sand we'd found in Bud Bronson's trouser cuffs, and they showed us their findings on that. It was beach sand and it came from a beach within the New York City pollution area. It was a beach that was washed with salt water which carried a notable percentage of sewage and a notable percentage of industrial wastes.

In other words it was just such a beach as we had been thinking about ever since Gibby had first spotted the sand. It was a beach which Bronson could have reached and from which his body could have been returned in the relatively short time that had elapsed between his last having been seen at the first Mrs. Stewart's apartment and our picking his body up when we captured the station wagon. Any round trip between Manhattan Island and a beach that would be free of traces of sewage and industrial wastes takes hours, far more time than Bud Bronson had for his travels.

So much for the lab boys. We turned from them to the reports on what had been turned up by the drive to find Bud Bronson's trail. There were good cops on that project, too. If there was a single character in the New York underworld to whom Bud Bronson might have spoken the night before and the boys had missed him, it would necessarily have been only because the character had left town immediately after talking to Bronson. They had hit all the spots and they had talked to everyone. Everywhere the word was the same.

Bud had been around. He'd been places where he hadn't been seen for months, not since he'd picked up with that babe who'd talked him into going straight. Everywhere he'd been asking the same questions. He'd been looking for snatch artists. Nothing else, only snatch artists.

We ran through the reports and, one after the other,

they told us the same thing. Bronson had leveled with us. Before he'd come to us, he'd exhausted his own lines of investigation. Not one of the characters he could think of to suspect was available. He had accounted for the whereabouts of all the local goons with any kidnaping histories. The police inquiries had brought out the same opinion as Bronson had quoted to us. If a kidnaping had been done in New York that weekend, it had been done by newcomers or amateurs. All the regulars were accounted for.

The reports were admirably complete. They included the times when all the people questioned had seen Bronson. With one exception these times represented that period he'd told us about, before he'd come to us. Gibby pounced on the one exception. It was a character called Al (Little Lambie) Lambruzzo. Bronson had asked him if he knew of any new men in town. Little Lambie knew of no one. He had been busy and he hadn't had much time for Bronson and he had been too busy to notice just what time it had been when Bronson had buttonholed him with his questions. All he knew was that it had been well after 3:00 A.M. Well after 3:00 A.M. was the time that interested us. If he'd picked up anything further from his underworld channels, it would have been from a character the cops hadn't found or it would have been from Little Lambie, despite Little Lambie's insistence that he'd been unable to tell Bronson anything.

"Who's Lambie?" Gibby asked. "Why don't we know him?"

"We've never had him in for anything bigger than gambling. Floating crap games, they're his line. Bronson would have been scraping the bottom of the barrel when he went to Lambruzzo for information."

"That's where we are," Gibby said. "We're scraping the bottom of the barrel. Where do we go to find Lambruzzo?"

Nine

Since, like his crap games, Little Lambie had a habit of floating, it wasn't any good our trying to find him. Since he might be in any of a dozen places, the police could canvass them for us and turn him up. Going out after him ourselves, we could have given it the whole day and we didn't have nearly enough time to waste any of it that way.

That, at least, was Gibby's decision; but before that dreary Sunday had come anywhere near running itself out, nobody could have convinced me that doing almost anything that might have popped into our heads could have been more profitless than what we did do. We joined the squad that was working those temporarily disconnected telephone numbers.

When we came in on it that day, we were having our first look at the operation since the little we had seen of it at its very beginning. That first look, furthermore, was most encouraging. The boys had put the job on a beautifully organized basis and the material was being sifted thoroughly and efficiently. We settled in with the cop in charge, a fellow named Murray, and he brought us his control sheets and showed us what had been done and what was still to do.

What had been done was extraordinarily impressive. They had the records on all temporarily disconnected phones. Out of those they had sorted all those connected to exchanges that included within their service areas any stretches of beach front. Except for a few New Jersey exchanges in the Sandy Hook neighborhood, they were limiting themselves to those contained in what the telephone people call the New York Message Unit Calling Area. This area consists of all of New York City plus Nassau County on Long Island, and southern Westchester and a bit of western Connecticut on the mainland. There was no need for them to go further afield because anything outside those boundaries would have been beyond Bud Bronson's reach in the time he'd had for the round trip. It would also have been beyond the area of metropolitan water pollution, from which area that sand had come.

When I looked at the list of exchanges they had sorted out for examination, it was hard for me to believe that they had done much in the way of elimination, but of course they had. There is one hell of a lot of beach front in and around New York, but it is still only a small portion of the whole staggering total of New York area.

The exchanges the boys had isolated for study were:

Amityville, Axtel, Baldwin, Bayside, Beachview, Benson-hurst, Beverly 5, Boulevard, Browning, Castle, Cedar-hurst, City Island, Cloverdale, Coney Island, Congress, Curtis, Dewey, Elgin, Esplanade, Fairbanks, Far Rockaway, Franklin, Freeport, General, Gibraltar, Glen Cove, Gran-ite, Hickory 1, 4, and 9, Honeywood, Hunter 2 and 7, Jamaica, Kingsbridge, Liggett, Lincoln, Locust, Lynn-brook, Manhasset, Mayfair, Michigan, Neptune, New Rochelle, Nightingale, Olympic, Oriole, Owens 8, Oyster Bay, Pelham, Port Washington, Pyramid, Republic, Rock-ville Center, Rye, Sheepshead, Shore Road, Sunset, Tenny-son, Terrace, Twin Harbors, Valley Stream, Virginia, Walnut, Westmore, Woodbine, and Yukon 1, 4, and 7.

For all the elimination, therefore, you can see that was still a dampeningly large lot of exchanges to work over. At the point where we hit them they had moved on into the second step of their procedure. Out of the total of temporarily disconnected telephones listed to these ex-changes they were eliminating those which, by street ad-dress and map, could be located in those parts of their districts that were not in the vicinity of a sandy beach. Some of the districts, like Coney Island and Sheepshead, were virtually all sand. Others, like Shore Road, had long stretches of waterfront with only a small portion of it sandy beach. Still others touched the shore for only a brief stretch but ran way back into the interior.

Since this part of the job was being done with maps and directories, it was also eliminating a great many num-bers which on a purely geographic basis would have stayed in. While working the directories, the boy were spotting the listings of apartment telephones and dropping those out. On what remained they were following the procedure suggested by Gibby. They had the local precinct working on the elimination of phones that were in partially occupied two-or-three-family dwellings.

"We haven't been waiting for complete lists or anything like that," Murray explained. "As we go along on this, as soon as we've checked a number that we can't eliminate on the basis of the directories, we pass it on to precinct for their check. The precincts are working along with us nicely. Regularly they are coming back within the hour with any numbers we can drop out because they are in partially occupied, small, multiple-occupancy dwellings."

At that point Gibby broke in on him with a question.

"Hold it a minute," he said. "These partially occupied small places don't necessarily fall out. Let's say it's a two-family house. Precinct checks it. One half is occupied. The other half is empty. How do we know the disconnected phone is in the empty half? It could be in the occupied half and our kidnaper could be holed up there, having the whole house to himself."

"We're covered on that," Murray answered. "Most multiple-occupancy jobs are either in row houses or in semi-detached houses. Even when they are fully detached, they aren't isolated. The house next door is only a couple of yards away and the walls are thin. There's no more privacy there than there is in an apartment house. Mostly there's less. You can't carry a baby in and out of one of those houses without all the neighbors knowing about it and you certainly can't shoot two people without being heard by the neighbors."

"Unless you're in the middle of a whole row that's unoccupied," I said.

"We're covering that. Precincts are reporting on all isolated houses containing these phones. It doesn't matter whether the place is isolated because it's a single-occupancy deal that stands in a lonely area away from everything else or it's isolated because everything around it is unoccupied. Either way they're giving it to us as isolated and worth looking at."

"That's good," Gibby muttered.

"Another thing we're covering," Murray added. "Where we have a two- or three-family house with only one apartment occupied and a temporarily disconnected phone listed for the address, we're checking for any phone that is listed as being in service at that address. If we come on one where there isn't any phone listed as being in service, that will be a really hot one, but we haven't found one yet. Where there is a phone listed in service, we put a call through on it and check. If we hit one of those where we get no answer, we'd figure that as possibly hot, too, but so far on all of them we've had answers."

"Good," Gibby said. "As long as we're not looking right at it and letting it slip past us."

"It won't slip past us," Murray promised. "The question is can we get to it in time."

"It's going to be rough if we don't," Gibby told him. "There's only one other lead we may have that could possibly take us to the place we want and that's a small-time crook who's already been questioned without result. We're having him picked up and we'll make another try with him, but that isn't likely to give us much."

"No," Murray agreed. "The little ones—it happens they get brushed by something big like this—they're too scared to talk."

"Except for one thing," Gibby said, "and it's all the hope we have there. The boys who questioned this little slob didn't think he was scared to talk. He didn't seem at all scared when they talked to him."

"Sometimes," Murray said gloomily, "it doesn't begin to show until you've pushed them hard enough so that they're actually talking. That's what scares them, the sound of their own voice telling stuff about some mugg who's bigger and stronger and tougher than is comfortable."

"Don't we know it?" Gibby sighed.

We went on with the telephone number search. You will remember that when we first set it up it was before Bud Bronson's body had turned up with all that sand for us. The priorities then had been completely a matter of timing. The boys were to look at temporarily disconnected numbers, starting with those that had been disconnected just two weeks before and working back from there.

Those priorities hadn't been dropped. They were still operating in that procedure along with the geographical ones we'd figured out from the sand. Giving first attention to numbers that had been temporarily disconnected just two weeks before and working in both directions from there had seemed a useful approach when we had first set it up. As soon as we worked out the beach-house angle, however, it became almost useless. This was October, after all, and most of the temporarily disconnecteds in the beach areas that weren't just two weeks old weren't much older than that.

Everything we had under consideration was either actually within the city limits or, if across the city line, it was in the closely adjacent suburban areas. Most houses that close in are occupied the year around. Take an area like Coney Island. You might find it cold and grim in the winter, but the people who have chosen to live there for the cool breezes in summer are people who pay the price of those pleasanter summers by enduring the greater rigors of the colder winters.

These beaches in and around New York vary widely. They range from slum areas up to quite comfortable, middle-class stuff. Here and there you'll find a relatively small bit that is quite upper bracket, but that's the exception and there's less of that upper-bracket stuff each year. All factors are working together to push those who can afford the best in the way of a beach-front hideaway farther and farther out from the city. The better roads, the faster cars, the faster and more comfortable cabin cruisers, the steadily increasing air services, all make it possible to go back and forth between the city and beach at greater and greater distances. The constant increase in congestion in all areas of the city and its immediate environs, the growth of industrialization all around the city's edges, and the constantly spreading reach of water pollution, all make it steadily more desirable to travel those greater distances.

It had in fact just about reached the point where, in those areas we were looking at, anything you might call the grand summer place that might still have been in use would almost certainly have been an old family home that someone was keeping going largely for sentiment's sake. There was a time many years ago when, come October along these beaches, there would have been a great many grand houses that would have been freshly shut up at the end of the season with the family moved back into New York.

It hadn't occurred to me that there would be anything like enough of that sort of thing left in the present day to show up as any sort of peak period in the temporary disconnecting of telephones. That, however, was exactly what we had before us. The period in which we were most interested had been a good deal of a peak period. I remarked on that, wondering at it.

"It's not the old stuff," Gibby said. "It's nothing grand. Most of these will represent flimsy, little shacks, one- and two-room prefabs, stuff like that. A man gets himself a couple of square yards of land near a beach and puts something like that up on it. He owns that and he has an apartment somewhere else in the city. He keeps the little beach place just for summer use. He lives out there and he rides the subway in to his job all summer. He sublets the city apartment for the summer and makes enough on that so the beach shack is costing him almost nothing. He can afford to hold it empty all winter just for the hot-weather use of it. He's just shut it up and he's had the company shut off the phone service till he'll want it again in the spring."

"Yep," Murray concurred. "Most of them will be exactly that. About five years back I had one myself out at Rockaway. Had it with three other fellows. We were none of us married then and the four of us shared an apartment over in Jackson Heights. We had the shack for the summer and we'd live in it from May to October and, just like you said, we'd sublet the Jackson Heights dump. When I got married, the others got a new guy to come in with them and he bought out my share. It was the same when any of the others got married. There was always a new fellow waiting to come in on it. I don't know who's got it now, passing along that way, but they'll be four kids living in the old apartment and going shares on the shack just like we used to."

"We can throw all of that stuff out," I said. "I know what those shacks are like." I had a picture of them as they stood huddled together in solid rows along streets that ran back from the beach. "They're so thin-walled and so close together that you could do better hiding away in an apartment in the middle of a Manhattan housing project."

"Sure they are," Gibby said, "but if you had one along in a stretch where all the other fellows had shut up for the winter and gone into Jackson Heights, it could be just right."

Murray nodded. "We've been watching for that," he said. "I've been thinking about that shanty we used to have. It'll be like that. A solid row of them, all with phones temporarily disconnected, all empty except one somewhere in the middle of the area where there's a guy holed up with a baby."

"This shack you had?" I asked. "Suppose you locked a girl up in there and left her there. Would she have to wait till she could telephone before she could get out? Didn't it have a door anybody could break down, windows anybody could smash?"

Murray looked crestfallen. "I was forgetting about that," he said. "She can't get out of there till the telephone is back in service and she can phone for help. Those beach shacks wouldn't hold anybody for even a half hour. You could break down the door. You could break the window and climb out that way. You could pick up a chair and break through the wall if you wanted to."

Gibby threw his arms around me and hugged me. "Mac," he said, "if we crack this, you're the one who gets the medal. Now we've really got it narrowed down."

"Sure we have," I growled, unable to share his wild outburst of optimism. "Narrowed down, but to what? Do you know? I don't."

"You've given me a glimmering, kid," Gibby chortled. "It takes just a little thinking and we can pin this down."

He did his thinking aloud and he did it step by step. I followed along and after a very little of it I caught fire. I had the impulse to jump up and hug him. My approach had been negative but it had opened a door in Gibby's mind and now he was charging through with a whole line of positive thinking. Dora Mason had been kidnaped. She had been held prisoner for several hours before she had been killed. During those hours the kidnaper had left her locked in the hideaway and he had gone out to make at least two telephone calls, the original one to the Stewart house and the one which Emily Stewart had taken in some phone booth so that she could report to the kidnaper what Hulon Stewart had said to the kidnaper's terms.

"Now let's look at this," Gibby said. "He leaves Dora Mason behind in any kind of flimsy shack. Dora is a big, strong girl. She's a girl who had both the heft and the spirit that it took to handle Bud Bronson when he stepped out of line. Why would Dora wait for the kidnaper to get back from the telephone? Why wouldn't she break down the door or bust out a window or knock down a wall? She would have been out of there long before he got through one of those long and impressive talks he had with Emily."

"No," I said. "You're leaving out at least two completely reasonable possibilities. If he has the Stewarts watched all the time he's holding the child—and the things he's known to tell Emily do indicate that—then this is not a one-man job. We don't know how many there will be in the gang, but we can't assume that he goes to the phone and leaves Dora unguarded. One of them stays behind with Dora and keeps her in order or else he binds and gags her each time he has to leave her."

Gibby interrupted. The first of my possibilities he did allow. The second he threw out. He reminded me that the ME's report had said no indication of binding or gagging on Dora's body.

"All right," I said. "She wasn't bound and gagged but there's another reason she would have stayed and waited for him to come back. He took the baby to the phone with him. Would she take off and leave the baby in his hands?"

Gibby thought she might well have done that although he conceded that it could have been a difficult choice for the girl. In any event, it was a consideration which, he said, we could forget about. We could focus on the part of the plan that involved leaving Dora and Emily prisoners with Little Lonnie while the kidnaper or kidnapers made a good getaway. Crucial to that part of the plan was this business of the girls' having no way of getting out or of getting help except by telephone and of being forced to wait for that until service was restored on the line.

"Come that time," he said, "they were to be alone. Nobody to watch them. Kidnaper or kidnapers, no matter how many, are all making that getaway. He is confident that the women can't make themselves heard outside the place where he's going to leave them confined and he is confident that they can't break out of it. Suppose we visualize on that basis. What sort of place does it have to be?"

We visualized. It would have to be a room with a strong door set in a strong frame in a stout wall. It would have to be a room without windows or with windows that were securely barred.

"It's a basement room," Gibby said. "Something down in a cellar."

"Which rules out any kind of a beach shack," I added.

"It rules out any kind of a beach house, even a big one," Murray said gloomily. "You're not going to find any house on any beach anywhere that has any sort of basement or cellar. You can't dig a dry basement along a beach. Actually you do the opposite. You set your house on a raised foundation to keep the wet out of it."

I groaned. "We're nowhere, Gibby," I said. "Murray's right. What have you ever seen along a beach that's the kind of heavy building we're picturing unless it's a lighthouse and that's too fantastic."

"Much too fantastic," Gibby agreed. "We can throw out more than half the exchanges we've been working on."

"We can throw out all of them," I said. "Take it from another angle. Where would anybody go to find a cellar with a telephone in it?"

Gibby told me. He came up with all sorts of places that might have telephones in their basements.

"Rumpus rooms," he said. "Who has a basement today without turning it into a rumpus room? A rumpus room with a telephone extension in it is a perfectly good possibility. Then there are horse parlors. You can't make book without telephones and there's no better place for an illegal horse parlor than in a basement."

"But not in a beach house, Mr. Gibson," Murray insisted. "Beach houses don't have basements."

"We have that sand," Gibby said.

"And Bronson picked that up on a beach," Murray conceded, "but then he went some place away from the beach and got shot."

"If he did that," Gibby said, "we have nothing to go on. We go on what we do have, on the assumption that the place is along a beach."

"We're going on another assumption as well," I told him. "We're going on the assumption that all the stuff about the disconnected phone isn't a lot of guff. What's to say that it isn't a beach house after all and there isn't any telephone there after all?"

"Hey, Mac," Gibby said, starting to laugh. "Hold it. Let's have some logic in this. We've just come up with the realization that beach shacks don't have rooms in them that are difficult to break out of. We haven't come to any conclusion that says they don't have telephones."

"I'm thinking of a beach house that doesn't have either," I explained. "Or I'm thinking of a beach house that does have a telephone but these kidnapers haven't bothered about having it disconnected. He wants the girl to come with the ransom money and he wants her to come alone and he wants all that without any police surveillance or interference. He can't persuade her to take the risk unless he demonstrates to her satisfaction that he has worked out some sort of getaway for himself and that he can manage without harming her. He builds up for her this whole tale about the secure room where he'll leave her locked up and the phone that will go into service after about a day or two and that way he sells her."

Murray picked it up. "You have something, sir," he said. "He sells the girl, but this stuff he's fed her is all a crock. We know it's a crock because we know they're in a beach house and there's no place in a beach house where he could lock her up and know she wouldn't be able to break out. There's nothing to any of it except that it's a way of getting her to take her chances on him. When she comes with that ransom, he isn't going to do any of what he's been saying he'll do. They'll either leave her bound and gagged or else they'll kill her the way they killed that other girl and Bronson."

Gibby surveyed the both of us with an impartial look of disgust. "Negative thinking," he said. "Defeatist. I've been considering all of that and there's no basis on which any of us can say it won't be that way. If it is, then we've got nothing and no help for it. We have to play the one chance we do have, if only because we have nothing else. We assume this bastard was leveling with the Stewart girl and we do have a chance of an entry into this by way of the temporarily disconnected phone. If our assumption is correct and we are lucky, we can still come out winners in this deal. If our assumption is incorrect, we lose, but we lose because the only line we had to follow wasn't any good. We don't lose for want of trying. We either work it out this way or we don't work it out. Show me a better approach and we'll hit it. The only alternative I see is that we sit here on our fat tails and cry, 'Woe is me.'"

He had us there. "I'm with you all the way on giving it the good try, boy," I said. "I just think we ought to know what we're trying for. A beach house with a basement?"

"Yep," Gibby said.

He was busily running down the list of exchanges we were working; and, checking them against the map, he was picking a few out of the lot to mark with red pencil.

"But there isn't any such thing as a beach house with a basement," I insisted. "It's practically a contradiction in terms."

"That's what I'm working on now," Gibby said blithely. "I'm throwing out all the beach house areas."

"That's everything we're working on," Murray muttered.

"Not quite," Gibby said. "The whole of the Long Island South Shore including the Brooklyn end—Sheepshead and Coney Island—that's out. You have too far to go from the sandy area before you hit any ground where you can dig a basement. The Jersey bit around Sandy Hook is also out. Same thing wrong with it."

We bent together over the list he was working and he explained what he was doing as he checked off his exchanges. Beach shacks and beach houses of all kinds were out. He was therefore dropping from the list all the exchanges that covered ocean front areas. He showed us on the map what he had left. There was a very small bit on the west shore of Brooklyn that had a stretch of sand along the lower bay. I remembered the place he meant and, as soon as I did remember it, I got the picture. It was then that I wanted to hug him.

That stretch of sand isn't more than ten yards wide at any point and back from it you have trees and grass and solidly built houses with cellars and basements and everything we needed. That Brooklyn bit was typical of the areas Gibby was retaining for consideration. There was that. There was Staten Island. There was the North Shore of Long Island. There were bits of the Bronx, Westchester, and eastern Connecticut where they fronted on Long Island Sound.

All these are areas with salt-water frontage but they are areas where the water has a mud or rock bottom and where even down to the water's edge houses can be built as they are built anywhere else, with solid foundations and as much basement or cellar as anybody might want. Here and there along this bay and sound frontage, however, there are relatively small stretches of sandy beach, but they are all rather narrow beaches.

The houses along these stretches are mostly built a bit back from the beach where good foundations can be dug for them, but you'll find a lot of them that stand only a few feet away from the sand. Picture Bronson. He has located the house. He wants to sneak up on it from the back. He's reconnoitering. He gets down to the beach and goes along the sand and approaches the house from that side. Gibby had it. All the factors were right.

The sections that remained under consideration because they covered both the sand factor and the basement-room factor were just those sections where you find the larger houses and the houses that are surrounded by plots of ground. If we wanted an isolated house that would be that close to a stretch of sandy beach and we wanted it that near Manhattan Island, we were looking in just the most likely places. Even if you've never seen New York or the areas around it, you can figure it out for yourself. When a man builds a house on sand, he may grab off a large area of sand to set it on but it will be only because he likes that much empty space around him. When a man can build just back from the beach and build on solid ground, he has every reason to spread himself. On three sides—everywhere but the beach side—he can have garden and lawns and trees. People are more likely to splurge on a larger piece of land than they need for a house when they can put all that on the land along with the house. Any sort of isolated house is a rarity in the New York area, but out around these fringes we're talking about they do happen. Furthermore they happen more frequently in these green areas that are edged by beach than they do along the ocean fronts which are all sand.

Gibby finished his elimination. "We're in business, boys," he said. "We drop out everything but these exchanges I've marked. Any numbers you come up with that are near the waterfront in any of these exchanges should be checked with precinct immediately and, before precinct checks them for anything else, they should be checked for sand. A lot of them that are right on the water will be like Shore Road in Brooklyn where you have pavement, a stone retaining wall, and then the bay and no sand anywhere around. No point in following through on those. It's the same way on the Long Island Sound frontages. Miles of that are mud bottom with small stretches of sand only here and there. Tell precinct that we don't want guesses or anybody's uncertain memory. If they aren't sure on any number you ask about, we want a squad car to go around and make absolutely sure that there is sand nearby even if it's a patch no bigger than a man can stand in."

We stayed with it and what had been looking like the faintest of faint hopes rapidly squeezed down to dimensions that looked very hopeful indeed. The list of numbers that had to be investigated was abruptly out of the thousands and down to the hundreds. Beyond that we had a good bet that precinct checks into the smaller particulars of local geography would rapidly squeeze out most of the remaining numbers.

If our lead was any good at all, we were coming within smelling distance of our quarry. I caught myself praying that the lead would be some good. Just watching that list of numbers dwindle to manageable proportions was like a shot in the arm. There was enough hope in the thing now for me to get eager. I got so eager, as a matter of fact, that when a call came through for Gibby and me, my first reaction to it was that I didn't want it.

The police had picked up Little Lambie for us. They were holding him. He was ours any time we wanted to talk to him.

"Let's go," Gibby said. He turned to Murray. "We'll keep in touch," he said, "but if you get anything that looks at all good, let us know immediately."

"Will do," Murray said.

"Why not stay with this, now that we have it panning out?" I suggested. "Let Little Lambie wait awhile. A little suspense might do wonders for his memory and if this works, we may not even need him."

"No guarantee that this is going to work," Gibby said. "We keep this going on the chance that our man wasn't lying to Emily. We get on Little Lambie in case our man was lying to Emily. Also we don't have so much time left on this that we can afford to let anything wait."

I looked at my watch and I was startled to see that it was after six. I'd had no idea that it was nearly that late. The day was gone. We had the night and what there might be of the morning before Emily Stewart would be starting out on her dangerous errand with five hundred thousand dollars, her courage, and what all too likely was a lot of disastrously misplaced faith.

We went over to our own office and the boys brought Little Lambie to us there. At my first sight of that character I had only one idea. I wanted to walk out on him and go back to our telephone-number operation. I've seen these muggs, all kinds and in all states of mind. For my money, Little Lambie was the wrong kind and he was in the wrong state of mind.

He was a lardball. There was a good three hundred pounds of him and all of it the color of lard. He had three chins and they were balanced by three rolls of fat crowded on the back of his neck above his collar. He looked as though he had two bellies. One bulged and sagged above his belt and the other sagged below it. His face looked like nothing human. It was a pig mask. The surrounding fat encroached so much on the eyes that they looked tiny and the whole area of his face was so much enlarged by the two annexes of flabby flesh which hung at his jowls that his ears and his nose and his mouth all looked as though they'd been designed for another face. It would have to be a face of more human proportions.

He was wringing wet and he was shaking visibly. The

police officers who had talked to him previously had reported that he hadn't seemed to be afraid. Now he was so frightened that he smelled afraid. You may not know what that is, but if you ever have the occasion to smell it, you'll know it. There's no mistaking it.

So it took no studying. Right at first sight I knew two things about this tub. He was stupid and he was frightened. Get them as badly frightened as that and still not talking under police questioning and it's obvious. You have a man that's too much afraid to talk. When they're like that, you can figure they'll be hopeless, particularly the stupid ones. There's nowhere they can go except deeper and deeper into fear and that gets them to the place where they're afraid to tell you what day of the week it is.

"Sit down, Lambie," Gibby said. "What's with you? It's not summer. It isn't even Indian summer. What makes you sweat like that?"

"Look," Little Lambie babbled. "Look. I'm clean. I don't know nothing. What's the rumble? What do you want?"

"You knew Bud Bronson?"

"Half the town knew Bud Bronson. Why pick on me?"

"He's dead."

"I know. The cops told me. They told me before. They told me now. I got an alibi. I got a sweetheart of an alibi, and everybody knows me. I never killed nobody. I never even hurt nobody. I'm gentle. I'm friendly. I like everybody and everybody likes me."

"You're the last man we know about who talked to Bud Bronson before he got it."

"I didn't even talk to him. I was busy. He talked to me."

"Same thing."

"It ain't at all the same thing. He's telling me he's got this broad and he says she's been snatched. He thinks maybe I know is there maybe some new people come into town. He thinks maybe I've heard there's something going that's real big dough."

"What did you tell him?"

"Nothing. I tell him to get wise to hisself. He's got a broad. Who's going to snatch his broad for real big dough? Where are they going to get it? From him maybe? He says that's his business. He say she's been snatched and it's for five hundred grand. Is there somebody new come into town who maybe works way up in that bracket?"

"Could you help him any?"

"Sure. I could help him a lot if he would only listen to me. I told him he should go around to Bellevue and turn himself in for a psycho. That's the kind of help he needed. His broad snatched for five hundred grand! What for a mishugass is that?"

"He talked to you and then he went straight out and found her. They're both dead now, Bud and the broad."

"The cops told me that, too. They said he come to me and asked me and he didn't know at all where to look for her. They ask me did I tell him where he should go look for her. I didn't tell him nothing because I don't know nothing. The way he talks, it's strictly from the filberts. He didn't go straight from me and find her. If he didn't know where to look before, he didn't know where to look after, not from me he didn't. If he got anything from me, it was maybe I showed him a little sense. A man pulls off a snatch he's looking to get five hundred Gs out of it. Whose broad is he going to snatch for that kind of dough? It's got to be a millionaire's broad, don't it? I asked him right out. I asked him is he a millionaire all of a sudden. I said to him I want to know because, if he's all of a sudden a millionaire and I ain't heard it, I want to congratulate him and maybe I can put the arm on him for a couple of hundred grand myself."

"I bet he split a gut laughing at that," Gibby said.

"No, he just hangs around a little while like he's thinking or something and then he takes off. You know what I think happened with him?"

"What?" Gibby murmured. "Please tell us."

"It's the same like I already told the cops. There's something with Bronson. It's made him flip. He's going all over asking everybody these same questions. I know maybe a dozen guys he hit like that earlier in the night, asking them. He didn't come to me because he thinks I know. He come to me because it's getting to be a habit with him or something. He asks everybody and he's down to me. I'm the guy who's least likely to know but he's asking everybody, so he asks me, too. You say I'm the last he talked to. I don't know. Maybe they's others. Maybe he did find somebody who knew something. I don't know, but what I think is when they flip like that sometimes they're not that way all of the time. Sometimes they have these spells when they're like me or you. You know, sane."

"He isn't sane now," Gibby said. "He's dead. Two slugs in him. Murdered."

"I know. I know. The cops told me already. But suppose he does get sane for a while. He starts thinking. He thinks Lambie's maybe got something. Nobody's snatched that broad. She's just gone shacking up with somebody else and, as soon as he starts thinking about that, he knows who it will be she's with. He goes over there. There's shooting. Now I ask you. Which sounds more like Bud Bronson? This, like I'm telling you, or this millionaire stuff?"

"What we have in the morgue," Gibby told him, "is the broad and Bud Bronson. We don't have the broad and the other man."

"So Bronson killed the broad and, when he shot it out with the other guy, the other guy got him."

"Both shot with the same gun," Gibby said, "and we know where the five hundred grand was coming from. If we want romance, we'll go to the movies. From you we want everything you told Bud Bronson."

"I already told you."

"Not enough."

"All I got."

"Try hard enough and you'll remember more."

"I been trying."

"You'll try some more."

"Okay. I'll try. Anything I'll remember, I'll go straight to the cops with it."

"It'll be easier than that. Just yell for the guard. He'll know where to reach us."

"You can't hold me."

"We are holding you."

"But you ain't got nothing on me."

"You're a material witness. Bronson didn't know where to go to get himself killed, not till he talked to you. After that he knew."

"What do you want from me? Want me to make something up?"

"That's too hard. You just remember. Remember and talk."

All he remembered for us was a flock of names, boys who had been in the game when Bud Bronson had come around bothering him. He remembered them with reluctance, just as any businessman will be reluctant to hand over to the authorities a list of the names of his customers, but he did remember them. They were a pretty waste of time. We found them. We questioned them and all we got from any of them was corroboration for Little Lambie. There were about a dozen of them and we talked to every last one. Of the group, five remembered that Bronson had been around and that he'd been giving Lambie a hard time. They remembered that he had been talking about his girl and about a snatch and they were certain that nobody had known anything or been able to tell Bronson anything. The rest weren't good for even that much. They had been too much concentrated on the dice even to have noticed Bronson.

We spent most of the night on those characters but in between we'd always go back for another go at Little Lambie. Each time we talked to him, he seemed to be in worse shape. If the disintegration of Little Lambie had been an end in itself, that would have been dandy, but that was not what we were after.

You know that old one about it's always darkest before the dawn. We had a variation on it. Dawn came and full daylight and we'd talked to everyone Little Lambie had given us and we were having him in for a last desperate go-around. We were covering the same old barren ground with him for the umpteenth time when the phone rang.

I picked it up. It was Murray, the boy we had running things over at the phone company. He had bad news for us. As I told you, when we'd left him, the list had been dwindling fast. It had gone on dwindling. He had called to report that the job was finished. We had dwindled right down to nothing.

"You've checked every last number and you haven't even one that's worth further investigation?" I yelped.

"Yes, sir. That's the way it stands."

"But it's impossible. Just overnight. You can't have done the whole list in that time."

"It mostly did itself, sir."

Gibby picked up the phone on his desk and got in on the line. We gave it a three-way kicking around. Out of the hundreds of numbers they had referred to the precincts, all but fourteen had immediately fallen out on the precinct check. The others were on waterfront stretches but nowhere in the vicinity of a single grain of sand.

"I've been talking to the various precincts about it," Murray said. "All through these sections it's winterized houses with oil burners and all the fixings. A beach shack is different. If you don't want to use it, that usually means it's a time of year when nobody wants to use it. These places are good the year around. Any time the owner doesn't want to use it, he can find a tenant. They don't stand empty with the telephone disconnected. So it works out. Temporary disconnects are just when the people go away on a vacation or something for a couple of weeks or a month or like that. It's long enough so it pays to disconnect the phone and it isn't long enough to be worth putting in a tenant. The reason we had so many for the whole area is because it's October and these people who have a nice, cool place for the summer months, a lot of them wait till late to go on vacation. They don't have to get out to beat the heat and they can go when they don't have to buck the crowds."

"I get it," Gibby said. "People with places right on the beach don't go away at all. They've got year-round houses on what amounts to vacation spots and they stay home and spend their dough on yacht club memberships and sailing boats and cabin cruisers and that sort of stuff."

"Right, all but fourteen who are away right now with their phones temporarily disconnected."

"Near sand?" Gibby asked.

"Yeah. I have it right here, the way they check out. Eight are in apartment buildings. Four were in a bunch. They are on yacht club property. You go in through a gate and there's a man on that gate all through the twenty-four hours. Also the deal is that the club provides service. So even though these people are away and they have the temporary disconnects on the phones, the maids have been going in every day and dusting around and like that. Nothing there, of course."

"That leaves two," I said.

"Near sand, with basements," Murray moaned. "They took longer. We got the report on one about fifteen minutes ago and the last one just came in. The first one is being painted and renovated while the people are away. Local real estate man's over there every day to see how the work's going. He's the agent for the place, good neighborhood reputation and all that kind of thing. Also it's an army going in and out of there all the time, electricians, painters, carpenters, plasterers, paperhangers, plumbers."

"That's Grand Central Station," Gibby said. "We can forget that one."

"What's with the last?" I asked.

"Tropical fish. We're down to just the one and it begins to look good. Sea Cliff. House on the edge of the bluff just over the beach. There's a flight of wooden steps direct from the back yard down to the beach. Not so isolated that a man with a baby wouldn't be seen coming in and out if he came by way of the street. This time of year though he could go the back way and use those steps to go in and out by way of the beach and he might get away without being seen. It sounds like just the kind of place we've been looking for. So the first neighbor they ask about the house knows all about it. The people are away for a month and they've got tropical fish. The neighbor is taking care of the fish for them while they're gone. She took the boys into the house and showed them the fish. She showed them all over the house. Nothing there."

"And that's everything?" I asked.

"Everything where the phones have been on a temporarily disconnected basis for anything up to six months. They were falling out so fast that we've worked them that far back, even though six months back is too long for this to have been planned."

"What makes it too long?" Gibby snapped.

"The kid's five months old, isn't he?" I said, knowing what the thinking on it must obviously have been. "It's just possible that this thing has been in the works ever since the child was born. Before that? No."

Gibby spoke into the phone. "How many do you have that go back more than six months?" he asked.

"Only four. There's one that's been carried this way for a little more than three years. That's the oldest."

"Where's that?"

"It's a Yukon number."

"Staten Island?"

"Tottenville. Do you know where that is?"

"Tottenville. It's around the far side of the island, toward Jersey. It's just this side of Outerbridge Crossing," Gibby said.

We were interrupted by a crash that shook the room. Little Lambie, all three hundred pounds of him, hit the floor. He had fainted.

"Subscriber's name?" Gibby shouted into the phone. "Address? If this isn't our baby, I'll eat it."

"Hold on a sec. I have it all right here."

We waited. Gibby was all one big, happy grin.

"Look at him," he said, admiring Little Lambie as he lay mounded on the floor. "Isn't he beautiful? He reacts like litmus paper."

Murray came back on the phone. He was reacting, too.

"Gee," he panted. "Maybe it is. I've been looking at these things and studying everything but subscribers'

names. I should have looked at that. The subscriber is
Emily Stewart, S-t-e-w-a-r-t, same spelling as the baby's
name. We'll check on that one right away."

"No," Gibby said. "Leave it alone. Just give me the
address. This one we're taking over on. It's ours. Leave
it alone."

Ten

We got the address and Gibby hung up, leaving me to give Murray instructions on what his men should do now. I told him to check out on the other three unchecked numbers he had.

"It's just for insurance," I said, "in case this should be a crazy coincidence."

I'd hardly put the phone back on the cradle before I knew that it wasn't a crazy coincidence. Gibby had been to the water cooler and had filled a cup and sloshed the water into Little Lambie's great, colorless slab of face.

Little Lambie came up yammering.

"I didn't tell him," he sobbed. "I didn't even know I knew. I didn't tell him."

Gibby threw some more water at him. "Knock that off," he said. "Get talking. What's the address?"

Eagerly Little Lambie came up with the address. It tallied exactly with the street and number we'd just had by phone.

"You're holding a piece of murder and kidnaping," Gibby said implacably. "Talk."

Little Lambie talked. He knew nothing about murder and nothing about kidnaping. All he knew was a dice game. It was a floating game which means it was held in a different place every night.

"Yesterday it was this place we been using now ten or twelve times a month," he said. "We been using it three, four months. It's this locked up house on the beach away from everything. You come off the bridge from the Jersey Turnpike, Outerbridge Crossing like you said. Then you go straight down the road and you turn off left and that's a road with almost no houses on it and what's on it has so much trees and like that by the road you can't see in to where the houses are."

Now that he was talking, it was pouring out of him, relevant detail along with everything that was irrelevant. Boiled down to the relevant, it came to this. Little Lambie had spotted the house. He had immediately been impressed with it. It was so isolated, well set back from even that little-traveled road. Between it and the road lay acres of grounds, thick with trees and between the trees overgrown with shrubbery and tall grass. There was more of the same behind the house but only for a few yards and then it was a strip of beach and the water beyond. The house was not visible from the road.

Little Lambie had gone in and looked around. Not far from the house there was an empty barn. Since the weather had been hot at the time when he discovered the place, Little Lambie had been greatly interested in that barn. He had made a few discreet inquiries in the neighborhood, a completely rural backwater out at the edge of the city, but at that Staten Island edge which of all the city's boundaries is almost the nearest to the city's center. It is a curious neighborhood. There is probably not another anywhere within the whole town that is as thinly populated and as sparsely built on. Little Lambie liked that.

He had pretended to be interested in buying the property and he had been told that it belonged to a rich gal who lived over in Manhattan and hadn't been out there in years. She had inherited it from her grandmother, and it was generally believed that, even though she never came near it, she would be unwilling to sell it.

Little Lambie was liking it better and better. Of all the various anchorages he had found for that floating dice game of his he had come to look on this one as his favorite. It was the most reliable and the most copproof. Little Lambie and his clients had been happy there.

He'd had the game out there one night early in the week and it had been scheduled there again for Saturday night. As was his custom, Little Lambie went out early in the evening, several hours before the scheduled time for the game. That was his practice. He was a careful man and even the best places could suddenly go wrong. It was a good idea to check and with a place as far from Times Square as this was he checked early so that he would have time to warn his people off and steer them to another spot if it should prove necessary.

Everything had looked all right. Nothing seemed changed and Little Lambie went in to get things ready for the first comers. As he came in through those nicely overgrown grounds, he had come on a station wagon. It had been parked far enough in so he couldn't see it from the road. He described the station wagon. Make and color and everything else he remembered about it tallied out with the job we had later seen when it had been serving as a hearse.

The station wagon gave him pause and he approached the house cautiously. It could have been all right, just a client who had come out several hours early, probably a nature lover who would be lolling on the beach until the play started. Then that hope died. He heard the crying of a baby and there was no mistaking it. It came from the house. He hadn't investigated beyond that. A client could have picked up that snazzy station wagon. A client could have been enjoying the beach till play would start; but no client ever brought a baby to any floating crap game. Damon Runyon to the contrary notwithstanding, Little Lambie knew better than that.

He pulled out fast and speeded back to Manhattan where he had an alternative site. Having checked that one and found it okay, he had hit the phone and passed the word. Staten Island was out. The game had moved.

"So you see," he said, "I ain't been lying to you and I ain't been lying to no cops. I'm busy. I got the game going and Bronson comes in and he's like crazy and wants me to stop what I'm doing so he can talk to me about his broad she's been snatched and all that. I ain't got the time for him but he hangs around and he's bending me my one ear while I'm watching the game with the other. Some of the cats they're in the game they're kidding around about how we lost the country place. That's what we called it all the time, the country place. And somebody says—you know, kidding-like—that maybe they ain't lost it. Maybe it's just me what lost it. Maybe this baby moved in and he's running his own game out there on a spare diaper. Then somebody else says babies don't run games and how it's a good place to keep a baby. It can cry all the time and they's nobody anywhere near to hear and knock on the radiator pipes. This was going on all the time Bronson was hanging around and trying to bother me. Then all of a sudden he ain't bothering me no more and I don't know when he left or what. He just pulled out."

"How did Bronson know where the country place was?" I asked.

"How doesn't he know it?" Little Lambie wailed. "It used to be Bud Bronson he was in the game all the time. It was him tipped me there's this place out there looks like we can use it. Staten Island, for Geessakes, how would I ever get way over there without somebody told me? Bronson he found it because this broad he had took him. They went there swimming and for a picnic on the beach. I went out and cased it and it was okay. So then Bronson was in the game out there a couple of times at the beginning before he stopped coming around anywhere any more and the guys told me he was really hooked with this broad. She had him on the wagon and working steady and out of the rackets and all."

It was perfect, but it was also crazy. We dig and dig on this thing and we have nothing and then, just when we touch bottom, the whole thing comes shaping up for us out of nowhere. I took to pinching myself. We'd come around to Monday morning, remember, and that made it that we had been a full forty-eight hours without any real sleep. There had been a little we'd taken in snatches on a couple of sofas in the office but that had been after our first go with Little Lambie, and each time the boys brought in another of his dice players, we'd been hauling out of it and pulling ourselves together to work that one. You can figure it out. It hadn't been anything like a night's rest. I had reached the place where I wasn't too sure when I was asleep and when awake. Getting a break like that, it could have been a beautiful dream.

We sent Little Lambie back to his cell. That was just in case we were going to need him some more. We checked with the Old Man. He'd had more sleep than we did, but he hadn't been idle. He'd set things up for covering the banks. He'd gathered in all the plain-clothes men he could muster and had assigned them around to the various banks. He was going to know it as soon as Hulon Stewart had picked up the ransom money. If Emily went with her father, the Old Man would know that; and if Stewart brought the money home and she started out with it from there, that was also going to be covered. A good stake-out had been set up for watching the Stewart house and the men were already on duty there. They were in an apartment across the street from the Stewart place. It was a completely safe deal, not a chance that the Stewarts or anyone else could know that we had set up that watch.

What with the men for Sixty-second Street and with all the banks that had to be covered, the Old Man had been digging deep into all the available manpower. He was able to give us one man, and we left it that the three of us would start over to Tottenville and, before we went near the house, we would check with the local precinct out there. The Old Man would be working on it while we were on the way out. He was calling the Richmond County DA, Tottenville being in that jurisdiction, and he promised that he'd have it set up so that by the time we got out there, we could expect full local co-operation. We couldn't ask for more.

We picked up our detective and took off. It was a boy named Paul Wagner. He'd worked with us on lots of cases before this. He's a good man. Since he'd had a night's sleep, he did the driving. We could have caught a little nap on the way out, but we were too hopped up for that. The way we went was down to South Ferry, by ferry over to St. George, and then down across the island to its far side over by New Jersey.

Going down the bay on the ferry, I had some grim thoughts about the sort of man we were going to find at the end of the road.

"This," I said, "is either going to be a lucky lunatic or a man with fantastic nerves. Can you imagine him taking that station wagon across on this ferry with the two bodies under the blanket in the back?"

"He didn't come this way," Gibby said. "It isn't the shortest way between Tottenville and midtown Manhattan and it would be the most dangerous. He went over the bridge to New Jersey, around through the turnpike and back into New York by one of the tunnels."

"That took plenty of guts, too," Paul remarked. "I know that road. He would have to stop three times to pay tolls, once for the tunnel and twice in Jersey."

"Guts," Gibby said, "he has. We've known that much from the first."

"Guts," I said, "and something like a genius for research. He'd learned that Stewart family like a book before he made his first move. He had the station wagon to use as an introduction for picking Dora up and he picked for his hideaway a place Dora knew. That was really something. He must have had her all the way to that lonely house out there before he even had any questions from her. The family had just suddenly decided to go out to that house of Emily's for the weekend. It was perfect for him both ways. If he used any other locked-up house, there would always be the chance that the people who owned it just might come out there at the wrong time. He uses this one. It's easy to sell Dora on it and she can't begin getting unsold before he has her where it's safe. That's one advantage he has. The other is that, once he's called Emily and made the ransom demand, he can be absolutely certain that none of the family is going to come down with any accidental notion that it might be a nice weekend for taking a run out to the old place. They would be having other things on their minds. He'd seen to that."

"And his disconnected telephone deal," Gibby added. "That was all set up for him. He didn't have to set it up. That was so good that it almost made us lose him. He has it figured that he'll call the phone company the last thing to order the service back on. He can do it from a railroad station just before he pulls out on a train. He can do it from a bus terminal just before his bus pulls out. He can do it from an airport just before plane time.

He can do it from any booth at the edge of town if he's making his getaway in a car. Emily wasn't wrong about this baby. He's a planner."

"Yeah," Paul said. "What I don't get is how a guy like him with his genius for planning could, when the chips were down, let his foot slip the way he did. Bringing Bronson back into town with the sand on his shoes. How stupid can a genius get?"

"That's in the picture," I said. "The boys who can plan an operation this thoroughly are the boys who fall into the mistake of assuming that they've covered every last outside contingency. When they run into the completely crazy, the completely unforeseeable, accident, their plan doesn't cover it and that's just when they do fall apart."

"He was a busy man," Gibby said, "and he just didn't notice the sand. Bronson obviously came up on the house from the beach. Our man caught up with him, but not until after Bronson had come off the sand to the hard ground. Not knowing that Bronson had been on the beach at all, this baby doesn't think of looking for sand. It's an understandable oversight."

"That poor, dumb Bronson," I said. "He gets this magnificent hunch. If he had only come back to us with it."

"It would have been nice," Gibby said wistfully, "but that was the chance we never had. What did Bronson have to go on? Little Lambie heard a baby cry in an isolated house that had been shut up for years. Maybe, because he was grabbing at straws, he would have gone out there on nothing more than that, but he did have more. He had just been up to Susan Stewart's place and we can guess the kind of picture he had from that. There's an embittered and lonely dame who fills her days by picking up with any kind of character she can latch on to and she's latched on to a peculiar lot. Bronson's just seen them. He puts it together with the stuff Gloria had been yammering and puts that together with the word that there is a baby out at this old, locked-up, family house. This is no ordinary hunch. It's a fat one. From where he stands the rich and respectable Stewart family is involved in some sort of private hassle and they're pushing his dame around. The way he sees it, he has to believe that, come to a showdown between somebody like Bud Bronson and somebody like the Stewarts, we'll be on the Stewart side. He goes out there alone."

"I just can't believe that Gloria was right about any of that," I said.

"She wasn't," Gibby said. "We saw Susan Stewart. We talked to her. She isn't tough enough for anything like this and she isn't cool enough."

We kicked it around all the way across Staten Island. Out at Tottenville we found the local precinct station house. Some of the older cops had long memories and they gave us a little more than we'd previously had. The house was Emily Stewart's and she had inherited it from her grandmother—not from her Stewart grandmother but from her maternal grandmother. Susan Stewart had lived in that house as a girl and the old lady had lived there till she died. That had been three years back. It had been then that the house had been locked up.

"The furniture and everything was left in there," they told us. "A couple of times a year, there's this dame comes out and spends the whole day. She's an old dame. They call her Agnes. She worked for the old lady way back, but that was before the present owner was even born. When Susan Stewart, the present owner's mother, got married, this Agnes went with her. Agnes still works for her and this old Agnes comes out here and has one of those cleaning companies come in and clean the whole house. Then in the evening she locks it up again and goes back to Manhattan. She was out that way just this past week. Friday, the whole day it was. She won't be coming again until spring now."

"A house like that," Gibby said, "with furniture in it and everything else. Don't they have somebody who drops around regularly to keep an eye on it?"

"No. We go in to the place about once a week and do a check. It's just to see nobody's been breaking windows or like that. This old Agnes, when she comes out, she always drops by here and says hello."

There was no need for going into it, but it was obvious that, when Agnes dropped in to say hello, she would probably also leave something for the boys. We did tell them about the game Little Lambie had been running in the barn. They didn't take that in good part. They gave us the big deal about how few men they had and how big an area they had to cover and how they couldn't be watching everything at once.

"If they've been there," they said, "they haven't been doing any damage. We'd have seen it, and Agnes, when she comes out, she'd see it sure. When she was in here Friday, she said everything was fine."

Susan Stewart may not have been tough enough or

cool enough, but it did occur to me that when we'd talked
to Agnes, we'd found Agnes both tough and cool. I was
wondering whether I could believe that the timing on
this thing could have been so good that the kidnaper
moved in the very day after Agnes had paid her semi-
annual visit and with a week of leeway before any cop
would be dropping by. When timing runs that close, are
you going to believe it's an accident or do you call it
careful research? I wasn't certain we could call it either.
Minute by minute this thing was coming to look more
and more like conspiracy.

It was almost nine before we had all the boys briefed
and everything set up. We were going in with Paul Wagner and one local man. The rest of the locals the Richmond DA and precinct were putting at our disposal
were to be concealed at intervals along that lonely road
that led to the property. Any information the DA was
sending out to us would be going to one of the other
houses on the road. It was an occupied house and an arrangement was made with the people in it for a man
to settle in there and take calls. Setting up communica-
tions to that point was easy enough. The tricky part of
it would be between there and that area close in to the
house where we would be operating.

Gibby had had a brain wave on that one. He asked
for a boat.

"Any kind of a dependable motor launch will do it,"
he said. "I don't want a police boat. It has to look like
somebody just out fishing or fooling around on the water.
Any time you have to get us the word on anything, just
send the boat out off shore past the Stewart beach. We

don't want any signals. Just let it come past. We'll see it and one of us will come out to the telephone."

The boat was provided. It was a little cabin cruiser called the *Suzy Q*. Nothing could have looked less like police business. We came down the road, dropping men off and checking their concealment as we went. We didn't go all the way to the driveway that led in to the Stewart house. Two houses before we came to that, the local man led us off the road. Everything up to that point was exactly as Little Lambie had described it, but there was something he hadn't mentioned. That house was even more isolated than we had pictured.

At the spot where we left the road there wasn't anything one would call a house. It was a jungle of a place and buried in it was the charred remnant of what had once been a house. We went in, penetrating almost as far as the strip of beach that ran along at the end of all these places. We didn't go down to the sand because in the bright morning light we'd have nothing in the way of concealment down there. We went only far enough so that through that last screen of trees and shrubbery we could see out to the water. We had to be in position to spot the *Suzy Q* if she came down the line.

Going along just there, near the beach but far enough in to be screened from sight, we worked past another house. This one was standing, but it looked abandoned and in an advanced state of disrepair.

"It's the next place after this," the local man whispered.

We nodded and began moving even more cautiously. I looked at my watch. It was a quarter after nine. Working slowly and silently through all that heavily overgrown stuff, it took us the better part of a half hour to come to the end of it. By that time we were on Emily Stewart's property and between us and the house lay a relatively open space. It was what should have been a stretch of lawn but there hadn't been any grass cut on it all summer and probably for a couple of summers back. The grass stood about waist high.

We stopped there and waited. Offshore there was no sign of the *Suzy Q.* We stood in our concealment and studied the house. It had the blank face of a place that is locked up and empty. The windows glistened in the morning light, evidence of Agnes' visit two days before. I studied those windows, hoping to catch some shadow of movement behind one of them, but there was nothing to see. We waited.

"Window," the local man murmured. "There's just the one basement window you can see because the grass in front of it has been trampled and it's flattened enough so you can see through to the window. That one's open. It's been pulled down from the top. The glass shines only in the lower half, not above."

I looked for it and I spotted it. I watched it till my eyes hurt. It was just the window as the officer had described it. Nothing showed. Nothing moved. I looked at my watch again. It was only a quarter of ten. We had been waiting there no more than five minutes. It had seemed much longer.

Then it came. It was faint and thin, but it was unmistakable. It was a baby crying.

"The kid," I whispered, "hear him?"

Gibby chuckled. "He's in good shape," he said. "When they cry like that, they're healthy. It's only the distance that makes it sound so weak. It's a longer stretch to the house than it looks."

"I can get you in closer around on the other side," the local man offered.

"No good," Gibby said. "From the other side we won't be able to see either the window or the door. We don't want to miss anybody who's coming out."

The *Suzy Q* came put-putting past the beach. Paul Wagner took off to pick up the message. He didn't bother about any of that slow caution we'd used coming in. He just kept out of sight. Any noise he made crashing through that straggly shrubbery didn't matter. We knew now that it wouldn't carry to the house. We had a check on that through the faintness of the child's crying. While Paul was gone, the crying stopped. It didn't drift off or anything like that. It stopped short as though a lid had come down on it and shut it off.

"What's he done to the kid now?" I gasped.

Gibby laughed at me. "He's given him a bottle," he said. "The timing is just about right since the kid started crying. It takes just about that long to get a bottle warmed."

"How long we going to wait?" the local man asked.

"We can afford to wait," Gibby told him. "He'll be coming out to go to the telephone. We'll have a chance to study him on the way out and we can take him on the way back. We're doing too well to spoil it now. When we take him, it has to be fast enough so he has no chance to do anything to the kid."

Paul came back to us. He'd been only about ten minutes, coming and going. It made that much difference not worrying about noise. He looked troubled.

"Precinct man," he said, "talked to some guys that run a dog wagon down by the bridge. They're open twenty-four hours and they've got a phone booth. They say a tall guy with a dark suntan and his head shaved like this Yul Brynner, he's been coming in and using the phone. They never saw him before Saturday evening. But he was in a couple of times Saturday evening and four or five times during the day yesterday and last night and then again early this morning. He talks quite a while each time. They say between Saturday and when he first came in yesterday morning he got his face scratched somewhere."

"Our man," Gibby said. "What's wrong?"

"He doesn't come with a baby."

"Now that," Gibby said, "is interesting."

"The girl said he had the baby with him every time, didn't she? She said he let her hear it cry."

"That's what she said," Gibby muttered. "This gets smarter and smarter."

I thought so, too. A baby's cry over the telephone could, of course, be any baby or no baby at all. The kidnaper had prepared himself for the inevitable question: "How do we know my baby brother is still alive?" One of those little dolls in his pocket. Tip it forward a bit and nobody could tell its cry from that of a real infant, certainly not over the telephone. I had wondered about that. It had seemed a discrepancy. All that genius for planning and then doing a fool thing like going into a phone booth with a baby in his arms. Nobody was going to make himself that conspicuous. Also in a phone booth he could have gotten the baby to cry. How had he been turning it off? A doll would turn off.

"It's all to the good," I said, after I'd taken that load off Paul's mind by describing this doll gimmick I'd thought of. "Now, once he's out of the house, we can take him and not have to worry about what he might do to the child. He won't have the child with him."

"Unless there's more than one of them in there," Paul said.

"There's only one," Gibby announced flatly.

I liked the confidence with which he said it. I wanted him to be right, but I didn't have the first clue to his reasoning. I asked him.

"Everything indicates that he's handled this end of the operation alone," Gibby said. "If he had anyone to go out to the telephone for him, he would never have continued going himself when it meant putting his scratched face on exhibition. It's taking that extra chance and he wouldn't take it if he didn't have to."

"There could be another man," I argued, "and he could be incompetent for the delicate job of handling Emily on those calls."

Gibby shrugged. "That we'll have to chance," he said.

The *Suzy Q* came by again. I looked at my watch. It was after ten. Paul took off to pick up the message. I knew what it was going to be. Hulon Stewart had the ransom money. We were coming down to the wire. We waited for Paul to come back. He wasn't gone even as long as he had been the first time. We knew he wouldn't be. He'd set it up so he would be met halfway with the message, but still it seemed a long time. It wasn't. By my watch it was only a couple of minutes.

It was what we'd expected. The Stewarts had the money for the ransom. A new signal had been set up. The next time the *Suzy Q* came by it was going to mean that Emily Stewart had left the house with the money, the automatic next step. If there would be anything more than that they had to tell us, the *Suzy Q* would appear to be having a bit of engine trouble when she came abreast of the place where we were hidden. We would hear her engine cut out and then start up again. If we heard that, Paul would make another trip back to pick up the news.

My watch showed ten-fifteen when the door to the house opened. A man came out. He was wearing slacks and a sweater. He was deeply tanned and his head was shaved clean. In the bright morning light the scratches on his face showed up clearly. He was a big man and well built. He was young but not a kid. He was also an ugly-looking character.

He blinked at the sun and he stretched and yawned. Then he turned and locked the door behind him. I expected that he would head out the driveway toward the road. He didn't. He came the other way, toward us. He sauntered. He might have been anyone out for a morning walk, enjoying the sun. He stopped for a moment and picked up a stick from the ground. It was just a light piece of dead twig and he carried it with him.

He passed not more than six feet away from us going down to the beach. He was switching at his leg with the twig he'd picked up and he was whistling softly. It was an old tune. I recognized it. "I can't give you anything but love, baby." Going along that way, he sauntered up the beach. Nothing could have looked more casual or careless. A man out for a walk. We watched him through our screen of trees and shrubbery until he was out of sight.

"Okay," Gibby said then. "He's gone to call Emily. He's a happy man. He's expecting her to tell him she has the money and he'll tell her where to bring it."

"That's going to be the knockout," I said, "when he tells her to bring it out here to her own house."

"She'll like that," Gibby said sourly. "She'll think he's considerate in addition to being efficient and thorough. When he leaves her locked up with the baby for a couple of days, it will be so much nicer for her in a basement she knows."

"I didn't expect that he'd go by the beach," I said.

"That's smart, too," Gibby said. "If he runs into anyone along the beach, he can be coming from anywhere. He has that stick and all the fixings for a man out to take a little walk."

We gave him five minutes, time enough to get him well away. Then we moved in. I hoped Gibby was right in his figuring that there couldn't be another man because we stepped right out into the open and ran for the house. I more than half expected that shots would come zipping at us as soon as we showed ourselves, but nothing came; and when we'd made it all the way across the open area to the house, I began to think Gibby could be right. We didn't bother with the door. We'd seen our man lock that. We went to the basement window the local man had spotted. It was solidly barred, but behind the bars the glass was down. The upper half of the window was open.

We got down and looked in but we couldn't see a thing. It was too bright out where we were and too dark inside. What we did see was blood. There were some stains of it dried on the bars over the window.

"Bronson," Gibby said, "died here."

Moving close up to the bars of the window, he brought his hands together in a loud clap. It was as though the baby had been waiting for a signal. It started crying. Jumping back from the window, we stood against the side of the house, waiting and listening. The baby cried steadily and nobody came to do anything about it. After a couple of minutes of that, Gibby moved out into the open again.

"So that's all right," he said. "No second man to worry about. He left the kid alone."

We went around the house looking for a promising window. That was easy. We found one at the back of the house. It was a kitchen window and it was standing open a couple of inches. We pushed it all the way up and climbed in. The kitchen looked used. It was a cinch that Agnes and her cleaning crew had never left it that way. We didn't waste any time on that. We had the baby's crying to guide us and it was easy to find our way down to the basement.

The room had all the necessary specifications. At the foot of the stairs there was a door that was one of those solid and heavy jobs they don't put into houses any more. It had its hinges on the outside and it had a good lock on it. This guy hadn't been kidding. Emily would have remained a prisoner there until the phone service would have come in. The baby was bedded down in its perambulator and that was one of those big, luxury jobs. The room seemed to have everything Emily would have needed for her period of imprisonment. There was a lavatory right off it and in the room itself there were comfortable chairs and sofas. Either the Stewarts had never bothered to turn off the electricity or the kidnaper had had it turned on. There was a television and one of those little bar refrigerators. There was an electric hot plate and a coffee percolator, also electric. The refrigerator had all sorts of stuff in it, including milk. There was a telephone.

Most of that, of course, I didn't bother to observe at the beginning. The first thing all of us did was head for that baby. It looked fine. To me it looked beautiful. Paul Wagner, because he's a father, was more critical. He didn't like the way the kid was diapered. He picked it out of the carriage and held it in his arms. Almost immediately the kid stopped crying. It's one of those things fathers know, the right way to hold it.

Gibby nodded approvingly. "It's stopped crying," he said. "Do you know any good way to keep it stopped, Paul?"

"They like to be picked up," Paul said. "As long as I go on holding him, he won't cry. If it was anything else making him cry, like gas or he was wet or chafed or anything, just picking him up wouldn't stop him."

"That's your department," Gibby told him. "You get him out of here. You can use the road since our friend goes by the beach. We'll stay here to pick the genius up when he comes back."

233

There was a stack of clean diapers sitting on a table. Paul looked at them.

"Unless he's got more of these somewhere," he said, "she wasn't going to be able to keep this kid dry for any two days."

"Why not?" I asked. "There's a whole stack of them. Isn't that enough?"

Paul grinned. "That many?" he said. "This guy will run through that many before dark." He picked up a couple of the diapers. "I'll take him to the house where we have the phone," he said. "When I get him there, I can fix him a decent diaper."

"You do that," Gibby said.

We saw him out of the house with the baby and out to the road. I was breathing again. Paul would be passing the word. The man was to be left alone. He was to be allowed to come all the way back to the house. We wanted to take him there. Pick him up anywhere along the road and he'd try a mistaken identity defense. He wasn't the man we'd seen come out of the house. We'd made a mistake, picked up the wrong man. You know how it goes. It wouldn't have been much good because we had this mugg too many different ways, but we were in a position to make ourselves the strongest case ever and now there was no need to hurry it and settle for anything even the least little bit less. We'd recovered the child. That was the big step.

We locked the front door from the inside and we looked the place over for a good spot where the three of us could wait and be the surest cinch to take him when he came in. Upstairs there wasn't a really good place. The house was built on one of those open plans with archways between rooms instead of doors. There was more available concealment outside the house than in. We resorted to what seemed the obvious thing, tooling back down to the basement room. That did have a door and a decently narrow doorway. We waited down there.

It was a wait but finally we heard the key in the lock upstairs. We heard him come in. He was still whistling that tune and now it had even a gayer lilt to it. The world was his oyster. He was on his last lap. The Stewarts had scared just exactly as much as he had wanted them to scare. All that money was coming right at him. It wouldn't be long now. He had it made.

We got ourselves flat against the wall either side of the door, ready to take him as he came through. He was a cinch to come down first thing to check on the baby, except that he didn't come. He had other things to do and I couldn't for the life of me figure what. He was clattering around upstairs and he seemed to be busy up there. We had outsmarted ourselves and good. Not a thing we could do but stay down there and wait and listen.

We weren't worried about his getting away. That was covered every possible way. The boys in all the hiding places had their instructions. As he came back in, they would close in behind him. By now they would be hidden all around outside the house. They would have the place surrounded. We knew that.

There was nothing to worry about, but the waiting was rough. After a while I was ready to give up on his coming down at all. To hope that we could get up the stairs and jump him before he'd hear us was at least delusional and to risk his catching us when we were on those basement stairs where we would be the world's easiest targets was foolhardy, but he did keep us waiting long enough for me to begin to feel foolhardy. I had to keep telling myself that it took nothing but patience. He would be coming down eventually. He would be coming down to lock Emily in that basement room if he didn't come down sooner.

After twenty minutes of that waiting I gave up on his coming down sooner. I started concentrating on my watch, counting the minutes till she would be turning up. He had sauntered to the phone and it was a safe bet that he had sauntered back. He wouldn't have abandoned his pose to hurry at that point. Fifteen minutes at least it would have taken him to make it back after he'd finished talking to Emily. I counted fifteen and added the twenty since he had come back into the house. That made thirty-five. How long would it take her? It had taken us forty and we'd started from downtown Manhattan. She had been coming from uptown and, taking the tunnel, she could come by road all the way. That might actually be a little faster. Subway and ferry and bus? I thought of that and the hours it could take but almost immediately I discarded the thought. A half a million dollars in bills of denominations not so big that they wouldn't be easily negotiable was going to make quite a package. How would she carry it? In a parcel? In a suitcase? A gal with luggage like that would have to come by car.

We sweated it out and then we again heard the key in the door upstairs. I had another look at my watch. It had been almost an hour. This would have to be Emily. I admired the guts of the girl, letting herself in to her own house this way to meet a man who had killed twice and who had promised her that he was going to let her off easily. He was only going to lock her up for a couple of days.

We were holding our breath. We could hear him upstairs and he had heard the key in the lock just as we had. His whistling had stopped and for a moment he made no movement we could hear. Then he was running toward the door. They spoke but it was in murmurs. All we could make out was the sound of voices, not what they were saying.

We braced ourselves. This had to be it. They would be coming down now so he could lock her in the basement room. They didn't come and, as I strained to hear, I tried to imagine what could be happening upstairs. I told myself that I should have known he would be this cool. He would be examining the ransom money, making certain that it was just the way he wanted it.

The stack of diapers was on the table right in front of us. Holding my breath, trying to hear, I found myself fixing my eyes on those diapers. I remembered what Paul had said about them. We'd checked the refrigerator and it had seemed well stocked. Now I was trying to remember. That wasn't the usual, family-size refrigerator. It was just a small, bar-size job. Was it so well stocked? I wondered how much milk a baby needed every twenty-four hours. I couldn't remember great quantities of milk in that refrigerator. The more I thought of it, the more it came to me that there hadn't been great quantities of anything in there.

He had come back from his telephoning and he hadn't come down for a look at the baby. Was he coming down at all? He was up there with Emily and he hadn't provided what she was going to need for weathering out the wait with the baby till the phone would come on. Moment by moment, I became more and more convinced that we had outsmarted ourselves. He was going to kill the girl and why would he bother to bring her downstairs for it? We were downstairs. We had all those men outside, but in between them and us he had the girl and he had her where neither we nor they could do a thing about it.

We could take our chances on the stairs. He might get one of us but not all three, but would we accomplish anything that way except triggering him? Wouldn't the girl be dead before we could get up there and get at him? Which was our better risk? What were we going to do now? I started edging closer to Gibby so I could put my lips against his ear and whisper, but then I heard them right over our heads. I flattened myself back against the wall and I didn't move.

There was the pounding of his footsteps and the sharp click of her heels. I'd been wrong. At last he was bringing her down. We were ready. We had been ready for more than an hour. They were on the stairs. Emily was talking.

"You have everything I need?" she was saying, and I could hear the tremor in her voice and how hard she was trying to control it. "Enough diapers? He'll be unbearable if I can't keep him dry, darling."

"I know, Em." That was the man's voice. "I would

have given an arm for some paregoric but you know we couldn't have gotten any of that. Too unsafe asking for it in drugstores."

"I know, darling," she answered. "I'll be all right. I'll be watching the television and I'll know you made it because there won't be anything on the news about your being caught and it will be just the two days and after that it will be easy. I'll wait a week for the look of things and by then Gloria will be bitchy again. You know how long her gratitude lasts, and I know a million ways I can get under her skin. That will do it. We'll have a fight and I'll leave home. It'll be an elopement. Ten days all together and then I'll be on that plane and joining you. It's going to be wonderful. It's going to be worth everything we've been through."

"Darling," he said and they were just standing there halfway down the stairs and smooching.

We could hear them. They were kissing and breathing hard. It was Emily who broke it up but not before I'd begun to feel as though I was hiding under a marriage bed on the first night of the honeymoon.

"Behave yourself, Fred," she said. "If I thought you ever kissed Gloria like that, I'd kill you."

"If I had ever kissed Gloria like that," he laughed, "do you suppose she would have married your old man, even with all his money?"

"I believe you. Now come on. Lock me up. Go on this way and you'll miss your plane."

"I hate to leave you," he said.

"Don't be silly," she said crisply and she ran down the remaining steps.

If only that local man had been a good hand with babies, we could have had Paul Wagner down there instead of him. She came through into the basement and she saw us. She was on his side of the door and he could have reached her if he hadn't been slow. She screamed and ran.

That ape had tried for her and, when he missed, he showed right in the doorway. The man on the stairs zipped a shot past her and got him in the shoulder. He went down and we were climbing over him to get at the stairs. By the time we made it they were going out the front door. We had all those men outside but they would have their hands tied. They wouldn't know that they didn't have to worry about Emily getting hurt.

The two of them were in the car and shooting down the driveway when we came bursting out of the house.

"Get them," we yelled. "They're in it together. The girl, too."

We had our guns out and were shooting at the tires but we were losing them around a bend in the driveway. Men came up all around the place and opened fire. We heard the crash. When we got around the bend we saw them. They had piled into a tree and Emily was dead. He was hurt and he was out cold, but he was alive. We would have him to bring to trial. Having looked so extraordinarily ugly before, now, despite his injuries, he looked startlingly pretty. I could see what he'd been doing upstairs all the time we'd been waiting for him. He'd been getting that make-up off his face. He'd been changing his clothes. He'd been putting on the wig which had been thick enough to save him from a skull fracture. He hadn't planned it for that, of course. The wig had been to make him look like his passport picture.

"The boy friend," I said, "the one she couldn't see at home because he'd once been Gloria's. How the hell did they ever think they could get away with it?"

"They were going to elope," Gibby said, "and never come home again. That's what she thought. Even after he assumed she'd made a mistake and let something slip to Bronson and he sent her Dora's body and Bronson's just to make her pull up her socks and be careful, she went on thinking they were going to elope. He'd had smarter ideas from the first. Before he locked her in that basement he was going to shoot her and there would be nothing left to lead to him. He'd be off with the money she'd made sure would be unrecorded because she thought she was going to spend it with him."

"That cold-blooded?"

"That vicious. The way they were coming down the stairs he shouldn't have had his gun handy. He didn't know we were down there. So he didn't have it ready for us. Who else was there? Only Emily darling."

"You knew she was in it?" I asked.

"Knew?" Gibby said. "There's no way of knowing a thing like that. I did have it hunched but I had to wait for proof."

"How did you hunch it?"

"The kidnaper's genius," Gibby said. "Every time we came up with anything that might have been useful, she came right back with the way he had foreseen it and already had it covered. It was too pat. He hadn't only al-

ready foreseen it and already covered it. He'd also told
her about it."

"Like taking the baby to the telephone with him and
letting her hear him cry," I said. "That was to keep her
old man going. She made it up to meet the demands of
the moment."

"Yes," Gibby said. "Like that."

"How do you suppose he ever got her to do it?"

"By getting her to fall in love with him. She wanted
him but she didn't want to be poor. There was a lot in
it for both of them. For him there was all that money
and maybe getting back at Gloria for walking out on him,
a beautiful way of getting back. He'd hurt her and have
her husband's money, too. For Emily there was everything. She had been rich Daddy's only child. A new
young wife and starting a new family had put a big dent
in that. She probably saw the half million as what would
have been hers anyhow or part of what would have been
hers if it hadn't been for Gloria and the baby. On the
money side she thought she was getting some part of what
she thought she had coming to her. With it she was getting the man she loved who happened to be the one man
in the world she couldn't have without cutting herself off
completely from Daddy and his money. This was a way
to have both her man and her money."

"Of course," I said, "she didn't have any idea of
what she was getting into. It was just going to be an ex-
citing weekend with a happy ending. She'd never wanted
money that Daddy couldn't provide and she hadn't expected that the thing would run more than a couple of
hours. Daddy would get the money. She would bring it

out here to Wilfred. Wilfred would lock her up with Dora and the baby. Then he would take off his make-up and put on his wig and take off and she would wait till the phone came on and then she'd call home and Daddy would come and rescue them. She'd wait a week and then it would be a bang-up fight with Gloria and she'd leave home in such bitterness at their ingratitude that she'd never come back and there would never be any danger of Dora seeing her husband and recognizing him. Also Dora's description of the kidnaper would be sufficiently off by the make-up and the shaved head for keeping Gloria and Daddy from recognizing him as Wilfred."

"Yes," Gibby said. "He had the perfect plan. She'd keep everything safe for both of them and she'd be dead before she had time to realize that it was not going to be for both of them but for him alone. He would have gotten away with it, too, if it hadn't been for Agnes."

"Agnes?" I asked.

"Yes. Bless her. She chose a Friday to come out and give the place its cleaning. They had to wait till she'd been and they knew they'd be safe from her walking in on them. And they had to make their move immediately after she'd been so that they wouldn't have any of the precinct boys coming around to check on the place. That made it Saturday and that held things up long enough for Bronson to find out. Even there we have Agnes to thank. Bud couldn't have had his hunch if Agnes hadn't at some time brought Dora out here. Without that, Dora wouldn't have known about this nice, private beach she and Bud could have to themselves for a picnic."

"What beats me," I said, "is their going on with it all

243

day yesterday. Bronson had found him. The plan had gone that sour. Every additional hour they waited multiplied their risk. What made them hold out? Daddy could get up the hundred thousand. Why didn't they take that and run?''

"A flock of reasons," Gibby said. "Emily probably felt that she was already making a sacrifice in settling for as little as a half a million; but she wanted her man now. A girl like Emily couldn't settle for anything as piddling as a hundred grand. She'd grown up to think of that as poverty.''

"You think it was her decision to stick it out?''

"To a great extent. When he sent the Stewarts the two bodies, he wasn't certain that Emily hadn't slipped and he was showing her that he wasn't fooling. Once she got past that shock, she began thinking it was all to the good. Things looked safer than ever to her after that. Daddy had been wavering. He'd had half a mind to co-operate with us. The murders scared him out of that. Suddenly she had him just the way she wanted him, so why quit then? It may even have been part of Wilfred's reason for sending her the bodies. He may have been ready to settle for the hundred grand since he knew something she didn't know and that was that only one of them was going to have the spending of it. He could have been trying to shock her into lowering her sights, but it worked the opposite way. He expected that murder would scare her into taking the quick out even at twenty cents on the dollar.''

I got it. "Right," I said. "He misjudged his gal there. She had gone into this scheme for half a million and her man. She hadn't expected that there was going to be any need for murder. Now she was in for a lot more than she had anticipated and, more than ever, she wasn't going to accept any cheap settlement. Half a million had been enough to make it worth doing a harmless bit of kidnaping. Kidnaping and murder was a bigger deal. It should have commanded an even higher price, certainly not any cut rates."

"Sure thing," Gibby said. "It's good, upper-bracket, financial thinking, isn't it?"